Bram Eased Storm Gently Down onto the Sand,

kissing her long and hard. Her lips were salty, her mouth sweet with the taste of the marshmallows they had roasted. He could feel the birdlike flutter of her heart against his chest. Storm was warm, alive, yielding, and so much woman that it made him tremble with longing for her once again. She was part playful child, but also part proud woman who made no excuse for what she was or was not. He knew in that liquid moment that he loved her completely, unequivocally and forever regardless of the outcome.

LINDSAY McKENNA

enjoys the unusual, and has pursued such varied interests as fire fighting and raising purebred Arabian horses, as well as her writing. "I believe in living life to the fullest," she declares, "and I enjoy dangerous situations because I'm at my best during those times."

Dear Reader:

SILHOUETTE DESIRE is an exciting new line of contemporary romances from Silhouette Books. During the past year, many Silhouette readers have written in telling us what other types of stories they'd like to read from Silhouette, and we've kept these comments and suggestions in mind in developing SILHOUETTE DESIRE.

DESIREs feature all of the elements you like to see in a romance, plus a more sensual, provocative story. So if you want to experience all the excitement, passion and joy of falling in love, then SILHOUETTE DESIRE is for you.

Karen Solem
Editor-in-Chief
Silhouette Books

LINDSAY McKENNA
Red Tail

Silhouette Desire

Published by Silhouette Books New York

America's Publisher of Contemporary Romance

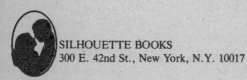
SILHOUETTE BOOKS
300 E. 42nd St., New York, N.Y. 10017

Copyright © 1985 by Lindsay McKenna

Distributed by Pocket Books

ISBN: 0-373-05208-1

First Silhouette Books printing May, 1985

10 9 8 7 6 5 4 3 2 1

America's Publisher of Contemporary Romance

Printed in the U.S.A.

Books by Lindsay McKenna

Silhouette Special Edition

Captive of Fate #82

Silhouette Desire

Chase the Clouds #75
Wilderness Passion #134
Too Near the Fire #165
Texas Wildcat #184
Red Tail #208

Silhouette Intimate Moments

Love Me Before Dawn #44

Dedicated to

The Coast Guard's brave men and women who risk their lives daily for all of us in the line of duty . . .
and
Commander Bud Breault, a former Red Tail Taxi Service pilot who did one hell of a job at the collective and cyclic saving people's lives . . .
and
LCDR Bill Nettel, Coast Guard black shoe, whose pride in the USCG is exhilarating . . .
and
USCG Air Station Miami personnel who made our visit memorable, impressing on us that their love and dedication is something all Americans can be proud of . . .

Red Tail

1

"You shouldn't be here, Lieutenant Travis," her flight mechanic said as she walked up to him.

Storm thrust her hands into the pockets of her light beige slacks in response to Merlin Tucker's growly greeting. The gargantuan helicopter and Falcon jet hangar was semiactive in the muggy Sunday afternoon heat at the Coast Guard Air Station in Miami. The sounds of mechanics working on their helicopters or jets filled the hangar. Only those who pulled duty were around. All except her. Storm drew to a halt, needing the familiarity of the sights, sounds, and smells to give her a semblance of emotional stability.

As she lifted her head and met Merlin's squinty blue eyes, a rueful smile pulled at her lips. "I guess I just wanted to be around something familiar, Merlin," she offered in explanation.

Merlin's triangular-shaped face screwed up into a frown as he observed her drawn features. "Yeah, I know what you mean," he said gruffly. "Come on over here. I'll show you what I'm doing." He looked around to make sure that no one else was near. Five other Search and Rescue H-52 helicopters sat like well-mannered steeds in their assigned positions on the floor of the hangar. Satisfied that no other knowledgeable mechanic was going to accidentally walk by and see his handiwork, he pulled back the cowling.

Storm wandered over, looking up at the turbine engine on the helicopter. "Are you sure you want me to see this, Merlin?" she asked him dryly. There wasn't another Coast Guard chopper pilot who didn't envy Storm when she pulled duty with the flight mech. He was the top mech on the base and everyone knew it. They said he had magic in his fingers. And when Merlin and Dave, her copilot, had been assigned to work together, they had always made an unbeatable team.

Her gray eyes darkened with recent pain. Oh, God, Dave . . . She had to push away all those nightmare memories. Wrinkling her brow, Storm leaned over Merlin's thin shoulder.

Tucker, who was only twenty-two, compared to her own twenty-eight years, chuckled. Everyone swore it was more like a witch's cackle. "Now, lieutenant, we'll just pretend this conversation didn't happen, okay?" He pointed proudly to the turbine engine on the helicopter. "I'm fine-tuning this bird for your next flight tomorrow morning. She'll pull a couple more RPMs for you when you need them the most." He grinned, the gap between his front teeth showing. It was against regulations to make certain finite engine adjustments because even the most experienced helicopter pilots who flew the 52s could overtorque the transmission and cause control problems. But Storm knew the absolute limits of the helo so he gave her the edge. His grin widened.

Storm turned her back on him. "I didn't see a thing, Merlin."

He cackled, rummaging back into the engine, grease smeared all over his long bony fingers. "That's right, lieutenant, not a thing."

Shaking her head, she gazed across the floor, noticing another person in civilian clothes entering the spacious well-lit hangar. A slight frown knitted her brows for a moment. Who else beside herself would be spending off-duty time here at the base? Everyone else had a family . . . someone to go home to . . . share life with. Stop it! You've got to stop this, Storm. It isn't going to do any good brooding about the past. You've got enough to worry about now.

"Why don't you take your day off and go home?" Merlin asked, capturing her attention.

Storm turned back around, resting her shoulder against the clean white surface of the aircraft. "Kinda lonely," she admitted.

Merlin surfaced for a moment, his normally gruff features softening. "Listen, lieutenant," he began, "it wasn't your fault. Lieutenant Walker disobeyed your orders. He should have stayed in the left seat. He had no business leaving the cockpit in that situation."

Tears scalded her eyes as she stared at Merlin, who was a couple of inches shorter than her own five feet eight inches. Her fingers trembled as she rubbed her forehead, a deluge of emotions surfacing. Why couldn't she cry? Get it out once and for all? The bitterness of the answer nearly choked her: because she was still recovering from the death of her husband, Hal, a little over a year ago. "I-I know that, Merlin."

Merlin grimaced and climbed down from the helicopter to rummage around for another tool. He straightened up, resting one greasy hand on his hip as he faced her. "Look, I've been in Search and Rescue for three years, lieutenant," he said, "and it's not uncommon for a drug smuggler to use any ploy or distraction in order to escape. That poor little kid just happened to be the bait. The smuggler was smart. Not only did Lieutenant Walker climb out of the chopper and try to rescue him, but so did those two Customs agents." He lifted his shoulders apologetically. "Lieutenant Walker traded his life for that little kid's. Quit blaming yourself because it happened. Hell, I'll lay you odds that if you had been the copilot instead of the aircraft commander, you'd have done the same thing he did!"

Pain was lapping at her temples again. She always got headaches because the tears wouldn't come. The tears just sat there, clogged in her throat, swimming in her eyes. But none of the animallike grief that clawed within her chest would burst forth, relieving her of the horrible anguish over the loss of her copilot and best friend, Dave Walker. "I went over to see Susan and the boys this morning," she said, her voice cracking.

Merlin's brows rose. "Yeah? How are they doing?" he asked.

Storm tucked her lower lip between her teeth, staring down at the concrete. "Not very well." She closed her eyes, drawing in a ragged breath. "They're like family to me, Merlin."

Merlin's blue eyes filled. "Yeah, I know they are, lieutenant. And you've become a part of everyone's family here at the base." He offered her a coaxing smile meant to raise her spirits. "I've been in the Coast Guard since I was eighteen, and I think the best thing they ever did was bring women pilots into SAR."

Storm looked up. Merlin was an unmerciful tease when he knew she was up for it. But one look at his open features and she knew he was leveling with her. She was one of three women in SAR at the air station. The other two women flew the sleek medium-range Falcon jets while she flew the helicopters. Merlin had been her flight mech off and on for two years and never said a word about this until now.

"What are you talking about?" she mumbled, brushing the unshed tears from her eyes.

Merlin grinned. "Hey, ever since you got assigned here, lieutenant, this place has really become a tight-knit family. You broke the ice, being the first woman pilot here. Not that we didn't have a family feeling before. But having women of your caliber around has made a real difference. We all took pride in our birds before, but when you got assigned to this duty section and I got to fly with you, everyone was dying of jealousy. And I mean envy with a capital *E*."

Storm forced a broken laugh. "Oh, come on, Merlin!"

"No, I'm tellin' you like it is. Now just stand there and hear me out, will you? Maybe I shoulda said something sooner. Maybe you need to hear this so you realize how important you are to all of us poor enlisted slobs. The way a male officer treats a situation is different from how a woman officer treats it. A man might bull his way through a situation that requires a little finesse. A woman seems to automatically sense that a softer word will do it better." Merlin grinned happily. "And I gotta tell you, lieutenant, we all like your touch. There ain't a crewman here at the base that doesn't love flying with you. They all know you're tops."

Storm felt heat rushing to her face. My God, she never blushed! Completely embarrassed by Merlin's sudden praise, she became flustered. "That's strange. I have a reputation for shooting straight from the hip."

"Yeah, you ain't one to mince words, lieutenant. But we all value your honesty. Just listen to me—what happened to Lieutenant Walker wasn't your fault. You're the best pilot here. You got a touch with a helo that no one else has. Why the hell do you think the commander is assigning the new guy to your duty section? He could have given you a seasoned copilot from another section." He gave her a satisfied look. "So there! You just stop and think about that before you start nose-diving again. Commander Harrison wouldn't be giving you a green copilot if he didn't believe you could teach the young pup the ropes of SAR!"

"Excuse me," a male voice interrupted, "I'm looking for Lieutenant Travis. Can you point him out to me."

Both of them turned as if they had rehearsed the synchronized movement a hundred times before. Their looks of surprise were identical as they surveyed the stranger.

Storm had to look up. It was the same man in civilian clothes she had seen at the entrance of the hangar earlier. Her heart took an unexpected beat when she realized he was staring down at her with more than passing curiosity. Myriad impressions cartwheeled across her mind as she took stock of him.

He was tall and broad-shouldered. Or at least taller than she; he was probably around six-one. His massive chest and breadth of shoulders told her he could easily carry the weight of the world around on them if he chose. Her gaze ranged upward from the languid grace of the hands resting on his slim hips to his face. Midnight blue eyes coolly met her inquiring gaze. His face was square, holding a moderately strong chin and a nose with a bump on it that told her, from the looks of him, that he had gotten into a fight at one time and broken it. But it was his sensual mouth with one corner curved into a slight smile that made her pulse race. It was a face molded by experience, with featherlike lines at the corners of his eyes telling her he enjoyed laughing. Lines across his broad brow broadcasted the fact that he concentrated unerringly on given tasks. It was a face hewn from more than thirty years of life and yet, handsome in an unconventional sense.

Merlin chuckled, appraising the stranger dressed in a pale green short-sleeve shirt and a pair of jeans. "Him?

This is Lieutenant Travis right here," he said, jerking his thumb in Storm's direction. Merlin chuckled again and gave Storm a merry look, climbing back up on the helicopter to complete the task of tuning up the engine.

Disbelief widened the stranger's eyes as he stared down at her. The sudden thinning of his mouth placed her on guard. Pulling out a set of papers from his shirt pocket, he opened them, the frown becoming pronounced on his brow.

"The Operations officer assigned me to this duty section to be Lieutenant S. Travis's copilot," he growled.

She wanted to laugh but had the good grace to curb her burgeoning smile. It was a commonly made error that she tolerated with ease. She was used to being an oddity among the male populace of SAR. And who was this man assigned to her? Commander Harrison, the Operations officer, had said a green pilot fresh out of helicopter school was going to be assigned to her. She had expected some twenty-four-year-old boy. Her gray eyes became somber as she stared back at him.

"I'm Lieutenant Storm Travis. Who are you?"

His eyes flared with utter disbelief. "There's got to be a mistake," he growled.

If he weren't so upset, Storm would have laughed. But right now his looks were turning thundercloud-black and she had no wish to provoke him further. In a gesture of defensiveness, she crossed her arms. "There's only one S. Travis on this base, mister, and you're looking at her. Now, who are you?"

He swore softly, looking down at the orders in his long spare fingers. "I don't believe this. Somebody's made a mistake."

Merlin peered across his shoulder, then ducked back to his work, realizing it was a safer place to be at the moment. If that big guy thought he was going to start giving Storm a hard time, he'd better watch his step.

Grinning, Merlin kept one ear keyed to the deteriorating conversation behind him.

"Mistake on what?" Storm demanded throatily.

He shoved the papers under her nose. "Here are the orders they cut for me out of helicopter school. I'm Lieutenant Bram Gallagher, the new copilot assigned to Lieutenant S. Travis's duty section."

Taking her time, she coolly read the orders and then looked up at him. What an arrogant macho male—

"No one's assigning me to fly with a damn woman."

Storm glared at him. "Too bad, Lieutenant Gallagher. The Coast Guard in all its infinite wisdom has done just that."

Gallagher stared down at her, fists planted on his hips. He had come in a day early before having to check in to find out the lay of the land. At Base Security, he had gotten his new I.D. and decided to wander over to the hangar area. This would be his new home for the next three years of his life. A woman? A damn woman was his aircraft commander? Of all the stupid, asinine things! He had heard the Coast Guard was moving to open more slots to females. But he never expected this! His nostrils flared.

"How many women pilots are stationed here?" he demanded.

"Three. And only one in helicopters. Me. Aren't you lucky?" Storm chastised herself. Dammit, she was behaving like a brat toward him. This wasn't the first time she had weathered grief from a stricken male ego bruised by her appearance.

He appraised her coldly. "There's got to be a mistake," he repeated unhappily.

Merlin chuckled and hunched deeper into the engine. Gallagher glared up at the flight mech and then turned back toward her.

"The only mistake is your attitude, Lieutenant Gallagher," she reminded him sharply.

Bram took a step back, trying to adjust to the shock. Under any other circumstance, she would have been worth looking at. When he had been walking up to where she and the mech had stood talking, he thought she had nice well-shaped legs. Like a willow, maybe. And when she had turned toward him, her dove-gray eyes had taken his breath away. They were wide and vulnerable-looking, with a hint of darkness in their depths. He had thought there was an aura of sadness surrounding her, but she had swiftly changed her expression, hiding her real feelings. Her nose was straight and clean; face square, holding a jaw that warned him she was nobody's patsy. Her mouth was decidedly her finest feature, expressive and slightly full. Just right to kiss. But right now her lips were compressed into a stubborn line, and her gray eyes blazed with silver flecks of anger.

In a characteristic gesture, Bram combed his fingers through his short black hair, pushing back several strands that always dipped across his brow.

"Look, I've just finished helicopter flight school in Mobile, Alabama," he stated. "I graduated at the top of my class, lieutenant. And I'm sure as hell not going to be relegated to a woman to help fine-tune my knowledge of flying SAR."

Storm relaxed slightly. At least he was honest. That was in his favor. She was glad to hear that he was at the top of his class. He wasn't a slouch at the stick, then. And judging from his penetrating eyes and aggressive stance, he was cut out for SAR. It took more than a very competent pilot, Merlin often told her, to fly well. It took guts. One wrong touch on the cyclic or pull on the collective, and mere inches could mean the difference between life and death. Storm smiled to herself. She liked Bram Gallagher's hands. They were long and artistic-looking, with large knuckles. Hands that proclaimed his flight ability. Almost every pilot she knew possessed those "flight hands," and she was no exception.

She grinned. Maybe she shouldn't have, but Storm couldn't help herself. "Tell me something, Gallagher. Why aren't you an ensign or a JG, coming out of flight training? You're a full lieutenant according to your transit orders." Besides, he was too old for flight school—past thirty. Her grin widened—two more years and she'd be over the hill herself. Suddenly Storm realized she was actually enjoying herself—at Gallagher's frustrated expense; but he looked as if he could take a few blows to the chin and live to tell about it. And her heart raced every time he gave her that look. It was a look charged with interest, ferreting her out, examining her, stroking her with his midnight blue gaze. She found herself drawn to him for no reasonable explanation she could think of. So far all he'd done was insult her.

His brows knitted. "Not that it matters to you, Lieutenant Travis, but I just happen to be an Air Force Academy graduate, with nine years of fighter pilot flying under my belt." He gave her a warning look. "And I was also a major in the Air Force, one rank above you before I left."

"Then what are you doing here?" she asked, disbelief in her voice. An ex–fighter pilot? This was getting more and more interesting by the moment. Even Merlin popped up and gave Gallagher an incredulous look and then dived back to his work like an ostrich sticking his head back into the sand.

Bram gave her a bored look, noting the confusion registering on her face. She wasn't pretty in a classic sense. Tall, yes. The ginger hair framed her face in a pageboy that barely brushed her shoulders, and it gave her an outdoorsy look. And she wore no makeup. That wasn't a detriment in his eyes. No, the natural golden tan of her skin made her gray eyes look like beautiful diamonds. Eyes that he could get lost in if he allowed himself to. . . . Shoving away all those feelings, he capped his torrid thoughts and brought himself back to her tart question.

"I was assigned by the Air Force to do a study on Coasties a couple of years ago. I got involved in your SAR flying and decided you guys had a hell of a lot more action going on saving lives than I did riding an F-16 around in the sky playing fighter pilot. I quit the Air Force and got a direct commission in this service and learned to fly helicopters. I don't know how I did it, but I only lost one pay grade. That's why I'm a full lieutenant and not a JG. It's one step down from major, in case you didn't realize it."

She frowned, immediately disliking his insinuating tone. "I'm not some child that has to be taught military subjects by you, Lieutenant Gallagher."

It was his turn to grin when he realized he had managed to probe beneath her cool unruffled exterior. So, she didn't like to be patronized. Good, he'd keep that piece of information under his hat. "Don't like the shoe on the other foot, eh, Travis?"

Glaring from beneath her dark lashes she muttered, "It's likely to be the other way round real soon, mister."

"Not if I have my way. Come tomorrow morning at 0800; I'm going to be in that captain's office asking for a duty section change. No offense, lieutenant, but I'd much rather ask you out for a date than have you as my AC."

Storm's lips parted and she felt heat rising to her cheeks. The nerve! She met his laughter-filled blue eyes. "Tell me," she spat out, "are all ex–Air Force fighter jocks the same? Overconfident male chauvinist—"

Bram laughed heartily, folding the paper up again and stuffing it back into his shirt pocket. So, she was human after all. Decidedly human. He allowed his eyes to slide across her tense form. Nice full breasts, slender waist, and beautifully curved long thighs. Not bad. Not bad at all except for that vinegar personality of hers. Still, she was interesting. Damned interesting. He'd never run across a woman like her during his service career. Well, maybe after he got his orders changed, he'd make a point of knowing her better. There was no wedding ring on her hand.

"See you later, sweetheart. No offense to you, but I'm going to go find a male pilot to train with. Women should be left to what they do best, and that isn't flying helicopters."

Storm gasped, openmouthed. Before she could find a decent derogatory retort, Gallagher turned on his heel, walking away from them. "Why—" she whispered angrily, "that—"

"I'll add a few more to that list you're making, lieutenant," Merlin said, extricating himself from the engine and watching Gallagher walk away. There was nothing apologetic in the pilot's stride or the way he squared his shoulders and carried himself.

She clenched her teeth, fighting back a few more choice epithets. "Arrogant swelled-headed jock!" she sputtered.

Merlin scratched his curly blond head. "Man, has he got a surprise coming. Old Man Harrison ain't gonna let him swap duty sections." He gave Storm a conspiratorial smile. "Cocky bastard's gonna learn his first lesson of becoming a Coastie—you get put with the best when you're training." He winked. "And that's you."

Storm groaned, pacing back and forth for a moment. "I don't know, Merlin. Maybe Gallagher would be better off with a man. At least he'd have more respect for him. Besides, I don't think I've got what it takes to put up with his brand of chauvinistic brutality right now."

The mech wiped his hands off with the rag he carried

in his back pocket. His face was serious. "Look, lieutenant, we'll back you all the way if he tries to pull any smart stuff. It'll be a cold day in hell if that bastard starts aiming for you."

She gave Merlin a weary smile. "Thanks," she whispered, meaning it. "God, when is my string of bad luck going to end?"

Merlin gave a philosophical shrug of his shoulders. "They say things always come in threes, lieutenant. First, your husband died in an accident, then Lieutenant Walker, and now it looks like you're gonna get saddled with a first-class know-it-all who's ex–Air Force and thinks he's better than all of us put together." He gave a sad shake of his head. "Well, don't worry, lieutenant. We'll be there to help you weather this."

Storm drove slowly down the avenues of Opa-Locka beneath the hot July sun. The city embraced the Opa-Locka airport where the Coast Guard station was situated. She had put down the top on her dark blue MG, needing the fresh air and the wind against her face. Anything that reminded her of freedom. She felt as if she were standing in a square room with the walls moving in on her. A cry uncurled deep inside her and she felt like screaming. But nothing happened. Her gray gaze darkened with anguish and tears pricked the backs of her eyes.

Bram Gallagher filtered back into her mind. She felt a moment's relief from the depressive grief and trauma. His arrogance bordered on the unbelievable. She had worked with pilots from all the various armed forces at one time or another. Fighter jocks all seemed to be cast out of the same mold—that raucous sense of humor, blended with a self-assured ego. Her own brother, Cal Travis, was a Marine Corps fighter pilot assigned to a naval carrier, and he personified those traits. And Gallagher was certainly no exception. Plus, he had the swaggering walk to go with it. Well, Gallagher, you've got a few lessons coming, the hard way.

Still, something had stirred within her dormant heart and Storm couldn't quite identify what it was. But it was a good feeling and, God knew, she needed something to neutralize the past few nightmarish weeks.

"Bram. . . ." The name rolled off her tongue. An unusual name. Different. And so was he. But he was distinctly male in every thrilling sense. A wry smile curved her mouth. "They ought to call you Ram," she muttered and then laughed out loud. "You just lower your head and charge!"

2

The first statement thrown at Storm occurred the moment she swung through the doors of the Operations Center. It was one fifteen in the afternoon and time for the next duty section to take the next twenty-four-hour alert. Lieutenant Kyle Armstrong was at the forty-cup coffeepot when she walked in. The other eight pilots raised their heads in greeting.

"Hey, Stormie, the Old Man's secretary called over here. He wants to see you right away."

She rolled her eyes heavenward as she joined Kyle, and reached for a heavy glass mug with her name on it. "You really know how to make a woman's day."

"Sorry," he demurred. "Hey, we saw your boy earlier," Armstrong mentioned, a grin lapping at the corners of his mouth.

Storm gave him a dirty look, throwing an extra spoonful of sugar into the coffee as a fortifying measure. "My 'boy'?"

"Yeah. The ex-fighter jock. What's his name? Gallagher?"

"Quit grinning like a damn coon hound hunting fox," she growled, lifting the scalding coffee to her lips. Wrinkling her nose, she took a small sip. Couldn't the day wait even long enough for her to get her customary coffee into her veins and wake up her brain? She had slept poorly throughout the night, finally sleeping soundly at eight A.M. The alarm pulled her out of sleep at noon, and she had rushed through a shower to make it to the station on time.

Kyle, who was twenty-nine and the father of two kids, laughed. The other pilots who were lounging around waiting for the orders of the day to be handed out joined his laughter. "Just a little inside info, Storm," he said. "Gallagher was over here at 1100 nosing around and asking about you."

"Yeah," Jesse Mason chortled. "He wanted to know *all* about you."

Her gray eyes narrowed as she turned around, observing her cohorts. She had been flying with all these men for a long time, and they were like brothers to her. "What'd you tell him, Jess?"

Mason, who was part of the duty section to be relieved, grinned. "Not a damn thing. Told him if he wanted to know anything about you, he should go and ask you. I told him how Coasties stuck together."

It was her turn to smile. "I'll bet he just loved that answer."

"Not exactly," Kyle chuckled.

"Hey," Jesse called as she turned to leave. "We don't want him! If the Old Man decides to transfer him to another section, Stormie, we don't want the bastard. He's too sure of himself. A guy like that can get you killed. I don't care if he was top stick in his class—his attitude sucks."

Chuckling to herself, Storm waved good-bye to

them, stepping out into the stifling grip of the hot, humid afternoon. Climbing back into her sports car, she balanced between shifting gears and drinking most of her coffee before she arrived at the Administration building. Now primed with coffee, Storm felt like she could withstand the coming showdown. Taking a deep breath, she entered the air-conditioned building and walked toward the commanding officer's quarters of Captain Jim Greer.

"Lieutenant Travis, come on in," the captain called as he saw her step into the outer office.

Storm entered the large well-appointed office, coming to attention. Out of the corner of her eye, she spotted Bram Gallagher. He looked breathtakingly handsome in his flight suit. And he wasn't looking happy.

"At ease, Storm," Captain Greer ordered, looking up from his cluttered desk. "I want you to meet your copilot replacement, Lieutenant Bram Gallagher."

Storm turned, offering her hand. Gallagher's grip was strong and firm but controlled. His eyes were cobalt with veiled anger as he met her mischief-laden gaze.

"A pleasure, Lieutenant Travis," he told her silkily.

Liar, Storm said to herself. Her fingers tingled from his touch as she resumed her at-ease position, hands behind her back. Greer smiled up at her.

"It's all mine, believe me," she murmured, barely able to keep from smiling.

"Lieutenant Gallagher has never worked with women pilots before, Storm. I've informed him that in the Coast Guard we're the least likely of all the services to be, shall we say, chauvinistic." He transferred his attention to the other pilot. "Storm will be responsible for teaching you all the finer points of CG helo operations, Lieutenant Gallagher. It will be up to her and the Operations officer to determine how much you fly or

27

don't fly. She'll help set up a training schedule for you, which will be approved by Commander Harrison, and you'll answer to her if there are any problems."

"And if there are, sir?"

"Then you talk to the Operations officer, Commander Harrison." Greer folded his hands, giving the pilot an icy smile laced with warning. "But I'm confident that if there are any problems, you two can work them out amicably between yourselves."

"We will, sir," Storm assured the captain heartily, flipping Gallagher a venom-laden look.

"Yes, sir," Gallagher mimicked, giving her an equally viperous glance in return.

Once outside the building, Gallagher reached out, pulling her to a halt. "You're enjoying this a little too much, lieutenant."

"Am I?" she asked coolly. Storm forced herself not to react to his firm, arousing touch.

"Yes, and if I didn't know better, so are your shipmates."

"You brought it on yourself, Gallagher."

His features darkened as he regarded her. "I've never seen men so protective of a woman in their ranks before. What'd you do, bed down with each one of them?"

Her response was instantaneous and totally instinctive. Storm's palm caught his cheek in a glancing blow, the slap sounding sharply. Startled, Storm took a step away from him, her face flushed scarlet. She stood there, hands clenched into fists at her side, breathing hard. Gallagher ruefully rubbed his reddening cheek. My God, she had never struck anyone in her life! She began to tremble from the surge of adrenaline flowing through her body.

"How dare you," she quavered.

A slight grin pulled at his mouth and he gave her a

sheepish look. "Guess I had that coming, didn't I?" And then his blue eyes darkened. "Storm's a good name for you," he said in a husky voice.

The suggestive tone was overpowering to her shattered senses. Storm was angry at herself for reacting like a woman instead of an officer who was supposed to be in charge. What the hell was the matter with her? Shape up, Travis, she berated herself. Her gray eyes narrowed.

"It's obvious you don't care for me as your superior, Lieutenant Gallagher," she told him through clenched teeth, "but that's something you and I are just going to have to suffer through. I don't like this any more than you do. And what's more, you had damn well better pay attention to my orders when I give them while we're in the air. The first time you even think of disobeying me could cause us to be killed. I won't stand for that. You can hate me on the ground but up in the air, mister, I'm the AC and what I say goes. Do we understand each other?"

Bram stared down at her. He lost his smile, aware of the steel backbone she possessed. The problem was that he liked her as a woman; already she had intrigued him. He had barely slept at all last night thinking about her. A new glint of respect shone in his eyes. "Okay, I can buy that, lieutenant. In the air, you're the queen. I won't ever disobey an order you give me—that's a promise."

She eased upright, realizing she had hunched over into an almost attacklike position. She stabbed a finger toward him. "You've got a lot to learn, Gallagher. You jet jocks in the Air Force are used to one-man shows. Here in the Coast Guard, we work as a close-knit team. In the air, I'm not the queen. I'm just part of the coordinated flesh and blood team that's flying that helicopter toward a rescue. And one more thing. All I want from you is your respect. Hate my guts, but respect the knowledge I've accrued." She marched toward her blue sports car, then spun on her booted heel, glaring at him. "I'll see you over at the Ops center. We're due for our 1330 briefing by the Section Duty officer."

What the hell had she done? Storm groaned, forcing herself to slow down on the way over to the hangar area. Her face was hot with mortification. I'll bet Gallagher thinks I go around slapping men all the time. Why should she care what he thinks? And that look Captain Greer had given her . . . he knew the fur was going to fly. She ran her fingers haphazardly through her ginger hair in an aggravated motion.

The ten Coast Guard pilots sat with their cups of coffee in hand as the SDO, LCDR Mike Duncan passed out the assignments. Storm sat rigidly next to Gallagher. She had endured his stare when he was the last to enter the Operations area. Storm had noticed that all the normal congenial noise died down to silence when he entered. A part of her felt compassion for him. He was new, and an outsider, not only because he was a green helicopter pilot, but because he was from another branch of the service. Grimacing, Storm glanced over at him. His probing blue eyes met hers. She quickly refocused her attention upon Duncan.

"Storm, you get to take those five loads of pallets from supply and drop them over at the staging area." Duncan, a man of forty with prematurely graying hair, gave her a slight smile. "Maybe you can show Lieutenant Gallagher the finer points of sling ops."

She nodded. "Okay." Great, they got the trash run today. Did she have a black cloud hanging over her head or something?

After being dismissed, Bram followed her to the line shack that sat near the Ops building. Bram came abreast of her and slowed his pace. Automatically

Storm allowed the rest of the pilots to amble on by them. She glanced up at him.

"What's wrong?" she asked.

"Nothing. Just wanted to apologize for what I said earlier outside Admin to you," he murmured. "It was a cheap shot."

She bit back "You're damn right it was." Instead she shrugged. "Apology accepted, Gallagher."

An elfin grin pulled at his mouth. "You have one hell of a right cross, lady."

It was her turn to smile as they walked down the sidewalk toward the line shack. "I've never slapped a man in my life. You were the first. And you'll be the last," she promised throatily.

Bram pulled the glass door open. The surprised look she gave him told Bram she wasn't used to that kind of help from a man. Too bad, he thought. I'm going to treat you like a lady whether anyone likes it or not.

All the duty section pilots milled around the cramped confines of the line shack. It sat next to the ramp area where serviced and repaired aircraft were parked.

Storm pulled over the maintenance book on CG 1378 and opened it up. Bram moved beside her, squeezing into the small counter space between the other pilots. She was vividly aware of his male strength, his body hard from being physically fit. Collecting her scattered thoughts, Storm pointed down at the log.

"We always check this to mark any discrepancies or problems with the helo, Bram. It's up to us to record them and then sign for the helo we'll be using that day."

The press of bodies, the good-natured gibing and jokes, filled the line shack. After signing out CG 1378, Storm shut the log, handing it back to the warrant officer behind the desk.

"Let's go," she said, giving him a slight smile.

Bram returned it, remaining at her side, and then

pushed open the door. The muggy afternoon air hit them as they walked around the corner of the building and onto the concrete ramp.

Storm began to relax. This was her home, the one place where she felt comfortable since the loss of her husband and Dave Walker. Merlin was waiting for them, over by CG 1378, throwing them the customary salute.

"Afternoon, Lieutenant Travis, Lieutenant Gallagher," he said gruffly.

"Afternoon, Merlin." Storm smiled, taking the mandatory baseball cap of dark blue off her head. Unzipping a large pocket on her left thigh, she stuffed it in there. The breeze was light, coming in from the Atlantic Ocean, and she inhaled deeply of the salt-laden air. She made formal introductions between Merlin and Bram Gallagher. Storm smiled to herself as both men eyed each other warily. She stood with one hand resting against the white surface of the helicopter.

"We want to welcome you officially to the Red Tail Taxi Service, Gallagher," she said.

Bram cocked his head. "What?"

Storm gestured to the international orange stripe that adorned the tail of their helicopter. "We're unofficially known as Red Tails."

"The taxi-service part is because you'll be doing anything from hauling groceries to rescuing snowbound families up in Alaska, depending on where you're stationed. Here in the Florida area we don't have to deal with snowstorms, but we fight the hurricanes every year." Her grin widened. "So if somebody calls you Red Tail, you'll know what they're referring to."

He scratched his head. "Relegated to a taxi service, eh?"

"Yes, sir," Merlin cackled. "Oh, one thing we forgot to tell him, Lieutenant Travis."

She gave Merlin a surprised look. "What?"

"Tell him that we're part of the Department of Transportation and not the Defense Department."

"Translated, what does that mean?" Bram asked dryly.

Storm pursed her lips. "It means if you get shot at by a druggie, Gallagher, it's not considered combat or even war. Since the CG is with the Transportation Department, we're an anomaly of sorts."

"A Red Tail and noncombat, eh?"

"You got it right, sir," Merlin responded. "An elite taxi-service with fringe extras like getting shot at." He winked. "When we stalk the druggies, we're in combat."

"Well," Bram said good-naturedly, "I was tired of flying a jet around all day. Looks like the CG is infinitely more interesting in many ways."

Maybe it's going to be all right after all, Storm thought. She went through the rest of preflight inspection with Gallagher, who became an attentive shadow at her left arm as they walked around the helo. He asked intelligent questions, and she was pleased. There was a new eagerness blossoming within her. Suddenly she was seeing Bram in a new light—as a professional pilot. When it came down to work, he was all business. The wisecracking guy with the arrogant chip on his shoulder had disappeared. Breathing a sigh of relief, Storm climbed into the right-hand seat, the AC's seat.

"Okay," Storm called, her voice echoing hollowly within the confines of the helicopter, "so much for social amenities. Let's get this show on the road."

A new palpable tension thrummed through the aircraft. Merlin busied himself in the back as they slipped into their confining shoulder harness and seat belt system after donning helmets.

Bram watched Storm out of the corner of his eye. Her movements were economical and spoke of someone who was confident with a job. He gave a small shake of his head. He was certainly going to have to change his perspective on how he viewed women. Because of the peacetime missions of the Coast Guard, there were women flying jets and helicopters and serving aboard the cutters at sea. A slight smile edged his mouth as he threw her a thumb's up, indicating he was finished with his personal preflight checklist. They began the next phase of checks for the starting of the engine and rotor engagement. Given Storm Travis's fascinating job as his aircraft commander, Bram decided to try and enjoy the time spent with her instead of creating a chauvinistic rift, which would only intensify the friction between them.

Storm adjusted the slender mike close to her lips, glancing over her shoulder to make sure Merlin was secure in his small chair, which was bolted near the entrance door. He was strapped in.

"If you'll call Tower, I'll lift off," she told Gallagher. "We've got five sling loads. I'll do the first couple of loads and you watch. Then we'll let you try your hand at it."

Bram nodded. "Fine with me, lieutenant." A glint of laughter came to his blue eyes as he studied her serious features. "Sure you trust an ex–Air Force fighter jock?"

She grinned back. "As long as you don't think this helo has afterburners, Merlin and I will survive."

Their laughter was drowned out when she flipped the starter button on the cyclic stick, which sat in position near her gloved right hand. The shrill sound rang through the hollow interior of the H-52 Sea Guard Sikorski helicopter. The trembling began and subsided as soon as the engine turbine came up to speed. When ready, she released the rotor brake, and the rotor slowly started moving around and around above their heads. Very soon, the steady noisy beat of the rotor smoothed out, and the 52 sat shuddering and trembling around them, ready beneath her capable hands. After receiving clearance from the tower, Storm placed her right hand on the cyclic stick that sat between her legs, wrapped the fingers of her left hand around the collective and placed her booted feet against the rudder pedals. Pulling gently up on the collective, the rotors punctured the air as pitch was increased and the ship smoothly slipped its hold from the earth.

Bram's respect for her increased as they worked throughout the afternoon carrying the pallets. The 52 could lift a maximum of eight-thousand-three-hundred pounds, including its own weight, so the pallet loads weren't large. He found Storm to be a natural instructor pilot. After watching her lift several loads with impressive ease, he tried his hand at it. The wind was picking up out of the northwest, and the pallets suspended beneath the 52 had a tendency to sway drunkenly from side to side. The helo's movement had to be choreographed with the temperamental load by constant manipulation of the controls. He grew to appreciate Storm's quietly spoken suggestions with an air of relief. Although he had been at the top of his flight class, six weeks to learn how to fly helicopters did not compensate for the on-the-job experience that all new graduates had to accrue out in the field.

"Anybody ever tell you you're an IP by nature?" he asked, glancing over at her.

Storm gave a distant smile. As always, her feet and hands were near her own set of controls. If Gallagher got into trouble, her lightning reflexes would have to save them. On any mission, the other pilot always maintained that position of readiness. "You mean I'm not yelling and cursing at you like the IP back in flight school did?"

Bram liked her husky voice. Her eyes spoke volumes. Her voice reminded him of a roughened cat's tongue stroking his flesh. It increased the air of mystery surrounding her. He knew nothing of her, and he wanted to know everything—especially now that he had had a chance to see her in action at the controls of a 52. She had what was known in their business as "hands." Another term used was "top stick." Even the IP in flight school didn't have Storm's silken touch with the helicopter, and it made him feel slightly in awe of her. She was a woman doing what he normally assumed to be a man's job better than any man he had seen thus far. He nodded, answering her teasing question. "Lady, if you had been my IP back in flight school, chances are I'd have flunked out on purpose, just to get another six weeks with you."

Storm avoided his openly admiring gaze, feeling heat sweeping up her neck and into her face. Oh, God, she was blushing! Compressing her lips, she looked away, forcing herself to concentrate on the task at hand. "You're doing fine, Gallagher," she managed. "Most copilots don't understand cargo sling procedures, but you're doing quite well."

Bram's grin widened. "Business all the way, eh?" he teased.

Storm refused to meet his eyes. He knew he had gotten to her! He had seen her face turn scarlet. "That's right," she informed him coolly, her heart beating traitorously in her breast.

His laughter was deep and exhilarating over the intercom system. "I'll let you have your way for now. But we aren't always going to be sitting in a 52, Lieutenant Travis," he warned her silkily.

Storm absolutely refused to blush again. She willed her body not to respond. Damn his cavalier attitude! Bram Gallagher certainly knew how to get under her skin.

"Hey, lieutenant, I'm starved!" Merlin wailed.

She glanced at her watch. It was almost supper time. Where had time gone? "Okay. We'll pick up this last load and then go eat."

"Anything the lady wants," Bram murmured innocently, but he looked meaningfully at her.

Storm ignored the implication. After the mission had been completed, they landed the 52 and shut it down, unstrapping themselves from their complicated harness system. Climbing out, Storm placed the dark blue baseball cap back on her head once again as did the others. Merlin and Gallagher joined her and they walked into the line shack. After completing his paperwork, Merlin went to the mess hall for some chow.

"Let's go up to the officer's mess," Bram suggested.

She grimaced, giving him a sidelong glance. "We could grab something from the vending machine. It's quicker."

Again Bram gave her that infuriating smile that threatened to make her blush. "Because I want to sit back and relax a little, Lieutenant Travis. Or are you going to give me an argument on that too?"

Her gray eyes narrowed. "No argument, Lieutenant Gallagher," she informed him lightly. Why did she have the feeling he was stalking her?

Stuffing her cap into one of the pockets of her flight suit, she walked through the doors of the officer's mess. They stood out in their olive-green flight suits among the other officers who were dressed in dark blue serge pants and light blue short-sleeve shirts. Storm bridled when she saw Kyle Armstrong and his copilot grinning up at her when they entered. She felt like she had to explain why they were over here and then decided to hell with it. Let them think what they wanted. They went through the cafeteria line, and Storm found a couple of chairs at an empty table to give them some privacy from prying eyes.

Bram sat opposite her, his tray filled. He gave a glance at hers.

"You're not eating much," he noted, pointing disapprovingly at the soup and salad.

Storm ran her fingers through her hair, wishing she had a brush right now. She knew her hair probably looked flattened against her skull after wearing the helmet. And then she laughed at herself—why, all of a sudden, did she worry about how her hair looked? She hadn't before. She met Gallagher's concerned gaze.

"I like staying at one hundred and thirty pounds, that's why. Don't start picking on my eating habits too," she said gruffly, picking up her fork.

His smile was devastating as he paid attention to his plate heaped with slices of hot roast beef. "Am I picking on you?"

"You know you are."

"My, my, aren't we touchy. Are you like this every day?"

"For your benefit, yes."

"My benefit?"

Storm glared up at him. She felt giddy and happy— but why? It was him. Damn! "Yes, yours. And don't give me that innocent look, Gallagher. You know what I'm talking about. We're not boy meets girl. We're adults. And I can see you coming from ten miles away."

He nodded, chewing thoughtfully in the silence afterward, his blue eyes dancing with laughter. "Want to play twenty questions with me?"

Storm gave him a black look. "No."

"What are you hiding from?"

"You."

"Why?"

"Because, lieutenant, you seem to feel it's your right to know me on a personal level."

He gave her a guarded look, continuing to eat. "I think that's fair. After all, we're going to be working together for at least a year."

"Don't remind me."

Bram grinned, knowing she didn't mean it. He saw the confusion and fear in her eyes and suddenly realized that something must have occurred in her personal life to make her so wary. "Okay," he said, easing up on her, "I'll can my twenty questions. Just answer two for me, will you?"

"Two?"

He held up two fingers. "Yeah, two."

She frowned. "I can count, Gallagher, and you don't need to hold up your fingers so everybody can see you."

So, that was it. Bram looked around, noticing a couple of the pilots and watching them with great interest. His face softened and he dropped his hand. "Looks like there's more than a little interest in you and me by your protective friends."

Uncomfortable and yet relieved that he understood, Storm blotted her lips with the napkin. He wasn't as insensitive as she had first thought. "They're worse than women when it comes to me," she admitted unhappily. Kyle Armstrong would tease her mercilessly tonight when they all got together at the Q or alert quarters.

He laughed softly, shaking his head. "What is this, reverse discrimination? Men being protective about you and on guard toward me?"

Storm shrugged. She didn't want to tell him that Armstrong and the rest of the guys wanted to see her married again. They were forever trying to fix her up with some eligible bachelor. Their hearts were in the right place, but it was embarrassing. "They mean well," she told him. "They're like brothers, you know? Sometimes they get in your hair and become an irritation."

Bram nodded. That was good to know—she treated them like brothers, not lovers. "Well," he informed her softly, his voice a vibrating growl, "don't even begin to look at or treat me like a brother, lieutenant."

She toyed with the salad, her pulse skyrocketing. "Don't worry, Gallagher, I'll never make that mistake with you."

His mouth drew into a grin. "Good. I'm glad we finally agree on something."

Storm gave him a warning glare. "I agree with you on very little, Gallagher."

"That'll change," he informed her darkly.

"I doubt it."

Storm didn't want to go inside the Q, which stood outside the ramp and hangar area. Four days had flown by and they were on alert again. It was almost 2100 when she walked outside, heading toward the quiet ramp where the readied helos and Falcon jets sat waiting for the next SAR call. Hands thrust deep in her pockets, she watched the apricot color of the sunset deepening. The colors were spectacular; she had come to love dusk in Florida. Tonight there were a few threatening clouds, mostly towering cumuli, rising like castle turrets in the distance. That meant a few isolated thunderstorms later over the ocean. Bowing her head, she walked slowly along the ramp area, away from the hangar, lost in the world of changing colors that painted the sky. It was lovely, and finally she halted, lost in the display.

"Beautiful, isn't it?" came Bram's voice from behind her.

She turned her head slightly, watching him quietly walk up to her shoulder and halt. The peacefulness of the sunset muted all her suspicions as she saw awe written across his features. He was just as moved as she was. A small smile curved her lips.

"This is my favorite time of day," she confided softly, returning her attention to the sky.

"Mine too. That and dawn. I like to see the colors on the horizon. Best time to fly."

She felt totally at ease with Bram. Four days had worked miracles in dispelling their initial distrust of each other. There was a tender look in his eyes right now.

Storm liked the feeling swirling and building quietly between them, a sharing of something far greater than themselves. The apricot hue deepened to an incredible orange that grew paler as it reached toward the darkening cobalt sky.

Bram glanced down at Storm. Her profile was clean, and her skin had a glow to it. There was a faraway look on her face now, and he longed to reach out and touch her. Her lips were slightly parted, her eyes wide, as she continued to watch the spectacle. They stood in silence another ten minutes before he spoke.

"I've been trying to find some time today to talk with you alone, Storm," he said, turning toward her.

Her heart catapulted as he called her by her first name. It rolled off his tongue like a caress, and she responded effortlessly to the tone in his voice. But she also heard the seriousness of it and faced him, a mere twelve inches separating them. Looking guilelessly up into his features, she searched his darkened blue eyes.

"About what?"

"You don't play games, do you?"

Her brows drew downward. "Games? No. Is that what you wanted to talk about?"

He shook his head. "No." He scratched his head furtively, looking toward the sunset again. "I'm having one hell of a time relating to you, Storm. You're not like the women I know. Or have known. They're into their cute, coy games. They don't come out and say what they really feel." He gave her a rueful smile. "You come off differently."

Storm felt defensive about his assessment, crossing her arms. "That doesn't make me any less a woman, you know."

He raised his eyes. "I didn't mean it that way. No, you're a woman in or out of a flight suit; believe me," he said fervently. Then he grinned. "The touch you have with a helo is a woman's touch, not a man's."

"Flying is a matter of finesse and sensitivity, not brute strength," she reminded him.

He held up his hands. "I agree. Listen, we're getting off track, Storm. I need to say something to you."

She licked her lips, preparing for the worst. "Okay. I always want honesty between us, Gallagher. Even if it hurts, I want the truth."

Placing his hands on his hips, he looked down at the concrete between them for a long moment. Finally he raised his head, an undecipherable expression in his eyes as he met her gaze. "First, I owe you a genuine apology for the way I behaved that first afternoon we pulled alert. I don't normally go around accusing women of going to bed with men." He grimaced, finding it hard to put the rest of it into words because of the avalanche of emotion boiling up within him. "Last Friday, before I left Mobile, Alabama, to move down here, I got my finalized divorce papers." He lowered his gaze, pursing his lips. "A two-day drive down here plus the bitterness of the divorce has made me a little sour on women. And when I met you Sunday and realized it was going to be a woman breaking me into SAR, I damn near came unglued." His blue eyes grew softer as he searched her stunned features. "I was angry at my ex-wife, and I lashed out at you instead, Storm. You represented all women to me in that moment and how much they can hurt a man."

Storm cleared her throat, unable to maintain his gaze. "I see . . ." she whispered. Tears came to her eyes, and it surprised her. Why tears? Her heart contracted with pain for him. "Under the circumstances, I guess I can't blame you for your actions, Bram. I probably would have done something quite similar."

A slight smile edged his sensual mouth. "I'm finding out all kinds of good things about you, Storm Travis. You stand up for what you believe in, but you're equally forgiving of other's mistakes. That's a nice attribute."

She shivered inwardly as his voice soothed her. Tears stung her eyes and she turned away from him. Was she going to cry? My God! "In the past year, I've found out just how human I am," she admitted rawly. Rubbing her brow, she managed a small broken laugh. "Just one thing . . ."

Bram cocked his head, watching her profile silhouetted against the darkening horizon. "Name it."

"Be just as forgiving with me, Bram. I-I'm kind of on an emotional roller coaster right now because—of, well, circumstances. I might shout at you when we're in the cockpit together, or—"

He reached out, placing his hand on her shoulder, turning her toward him. It startled him to realize that her dove-gray eyes were filled with tears, making them appear luminous and vulnerable. He wanted to keep his hand on her shoulder but allowed it to drop to his side instead.

"We got off on the wrong foot the other day because of my attitude, Storm," he told her earnestly. "You showed your professionalism with me, regardless of how badly I made an ass of myself. You didn't let your personal opinion of me interfere with teaching me the ropes. You've earned a big chunk of my respect. I'll never lose my temper with you when you get a little out of sorts."

A quivering smile fled across her lips. His touch had been healing and stabilizing to her torn emotional state. Storm longed to have him put his hand on her once again, to simply step into the circle of his arms. She had been a year without any kind of emotional support— bereft, floating aimlessly. And she yearned for what Bram offered honestly and without games. A newfound respect shone in her eyes for him.

"Okay," she murmured huskily, "truce?"

"Truce," Bram promised thickly.

3

The Q, the barracks for pilots on alert, consisted of two double bunks to a room in a two-story structure. On retiring to their rooms, the pilots unlaced their boots and left them nearby in case the duty officer called on two or more of them to assist in a search and rescue mission. The room at the end of the hall was a large lounge sporting several comfortable sofas and chairs gathered around a color TV set. Storm had her boots off, dangling her long legs over the arm of the chair. It was almost ten P.M. and she dozed intermittently, the television blaring in the background, providing the stabilizing sound of human voices.

One by one, the on-duty pilots called it a night. Storm was afraid to go to bed. This was her first night back on duty since the loss of Dave Walker. She had been placed on nonduty status and given time to recover from the emotional shock and loss. It was the normal procedure after air crashes or traumatic circumstances. Kyle rose and walked over under Bram's watchful eye, his hands resting on each arm of the chair as he stared down at her.

"Okay, Stormie?" he asked in a low voice.

She nodded, barely opening her eyes. "Yeah, fine, Kyle."

"Sure?"

Kyle knew what she was going through. They had been close friends since she had first been assigned to SAR. "Yeah . . ." she mumbled, her arms wrapped across her body, head buried against the chair.

"You look real tired."

"I am."

"Why don't you hit the rack? You're gonna end up with a crick in your neck if you don't." He smiled, but his green eyes were solemn as he watched her closely.

Storm shrugged. She didn't want to tell Kyle of the nightmares that stalked her every night. "I'll go in a little while. Thanks. . . ."

He straightened up, giving her knee a pat. "Okay. Good night."

Dozing again beneath the lamplight and the comforting noise of the television, Storm remembered very little after that. At one point, Bram came over and checked on her before he left for his room, which was situated next to hers. He had gently stroked her hair, crouching down beside her, his blue eyes assessing her worriedly. For the first time in a year, she felt protected. Smiling softly, she mumbled good night to him and dozed off again.

Near eleven, Storm roused herself and stumbled blindly into her darkened sleeping quarters. Drunk with exhaustion, she left her flight suit on and wearily lay down on the bunk. Maybe now she was tired enough for sleep to come without a battle. She was lucky if she got three hours of sleep a night since the accident.

"I've got to help him, Storm!"

She shook her head adamantly, gripping the flight

controls as the helicopter hovered precariously over the deck of the yacht. The ocean was fairly calm, making the boarding of the ship by the SES drug-busting Coast Guard crew of the *Sea Hawk* relatively easy. The yacht had a helicopter landing pad on the rear deck. When the request came in for them to assist in the mop-up operation, Storm landed the aircraft gently on the pad. It was an unusual request, but she complied. Merlin was out the door, helping to round up the smugglers and their cache of marijuana and coke. But it wasn't over yet. The whine of the turbine engine of the 52 added to the cacophony of shouts and orders. She and Dave watched in horror as one smuggler grabbed a small boy who was part of the crew, holding him hostage at the bow of the ship with a gun held to his head. Two Customs agents armed with shotguns slowly approached the twosome.

"He isn't going to put down the gun," Dave said grimly, giving Storm a sharp glance. He began unharnessing. "Damn!"

"Dave . . . don't go! Stay here. There's nothing you can do!" she ordered. Her concentration was torn between keeping the helicopter steady on the deck and remaining aware of the chaos taking place around them.

"He's gonna kill that kid, Storm. I know Spanish. Maybe I can get our guys to back off and I'll talk him into giving up the boy."

Before Storm could protest, he was gone. Helplessly she watched as Dave, still in his helmet, climbed out and ran toward the prow of the ship. She bit her lower lip hard, aware of the hatred on the face of the Colombian smuggler. Storm watched as everything in her recurring nightmare slowed to anguished single frames, sending waves of horror through her.

Even above the roar of the 52's rotor blades kicking

up gusts of wind, Storm heard the smuggler screaming shrilly in Spanish as Dave placed himself in front of the boarding crew. Her stomach knotted, and her sweaty hands tightened on the controls. The smuggler raised the gun, aiming it at Dave's chest. No! Oh, God, no! He was going to shoot Dave! She watched as the ugly snout of the gun barrel rose level with Dave Walker's chest. She saw the man's finger pulling back on the trigger.

"No!" she screamed again and again. Sobs tore from her throat, and she buried her face in her trembling hands, unable to stop the awful sounds from escaping. She was barely cognizant of someone switching on the overhead light, as well as the mumbling and movement around her. Hands, friendly hands, fell on her shoulder, pulling her around, breaking the spell.

"Stormie?" Kyle whispered anxiously. He pulled her upright so she could sit up. A few of the other pilots, awakened from their sleep by her screams, stumbled out of bed and down the hall, coming to her room and standing near Armstrong.

She sobbed hard, embarrassed, realizing she had awakened almost everyone in the Q. "I-I'm sorry," she cried brokenly. "I didn't mean to wake everyone . . ."

Armstrong smiled understandingly, watching as Gallagher made his way through the assembled pilots, crouching down by Storm's left leg. "It's okay," Bram soothed.

Storm felt Bram's firm grip on her arm. It had an immediate mollifying effect on her turbulent emotional state.

"I'll take care of her," Bram told the others, daring any of them to dispute his right to do so. She was his partner. He was her copilot. It was an unwritten law that they took care of each other, and it didn't matter how new he was. Reluctantly Armstrong released his grip on

Storm's other arm. There was a trace of disbelief in his green eyes, questioning Bram's motives. He glanced up at Storm, who was trying to wipe away the tears with her trembling hands.

"Stormie?"

"I-Bram will take care of me," she stammered thickly. "I'm going to get up anyway. You guys don't need me waking you up again. Especially when we're on alert." She rose unsteadily, grateful for Bram's assistance. Grabbing her boots, she stumbled from the room and headed toward the lounge. She found a chair and sat down, pulling on the boots and lacing them up expertly out of habit. Bram joined her moments later, his boots already on. His hair was tousled, his eyes puffy with sleep. She felt a sharp stab of guilt as she met his inquiring blue gaze.

"I'm sorry, Bram," she murmured, standing.

He shrugged his broad shoulders. "Don't be. Come on, let's go for a walk. You need some fresh air."

How did he know that? The confining area was almost suffocating her. She made no protest when he kept his hand on her arm as he led her outside into the muggy night. They walked away from the building toward the ramp in the distance. Once the darkness closed in on her, she felt better. Looking up, Storm lost herself in the beauty of the night sky. They walked for almost ten minutes before she finally came to a stop and turned to Bram.

"You must think I'm crazy."

His craggy features were shadowed by the starlight as he looked down on her. "No. I think something traumatic happened recently. I've known too many good pilots who had to bail out or lost someone in a crash to think you're crazy." A slight smile pulled at his mouth. "You scared the hell out of me, though. I probably rose two feet off that bunk when you started screaming."

Storm shakily pushed her slender fingers through her hair. "God, I feel like a fool," she muttered. "What will the other guys think?"

Bram reached out, placing both hands on her shoulders, his fingers lightly massaging the tenseness out of them. "They were worried for you, Storm. Want to tell me what happened? I'm your copilot, remember? We're a team now."

She was grateful for his gentle demeanor. His hands were strong and coaxing to her taut shoulder muscles, and she longed just to fall into his arms. Hesitantly she told him about Dave Walker. Tears welled up in her eyes again as she repeated the nightmare to him.

Bram released her, then lifted his calloused hands and framed her face, forcing her to look up at him. His heart wrenched in his chest as he saw the glittering gray diamonds of her eyes awash with tears.

"Look," he said evenly, "that was a situation where no matter what you said or how you felt, Storm, Dave would have done it anyway. If he loved children that much, you had to expect that of him. He counted on the smuggler giving up the child, not shooting him instead," he told her softly.

Huge tears rolled down her taut cheeks and Bram's features blurred. "But-but I lost my copilot!" she cried hoarsely. "I was responsible! I should have done something more—"

Bram's face tightened, his eyes darkening. "Listen to me, Storm," he said gruffly in a more authoritative voice, "you did all you could. You sat with a helicopter perched on a yacht that was unstable as hell. There was no way you could shut down the 52 and go out there to help him. The helicopter might have slid off into the ocean. You accurately assessed your duties." His lips became a grim line. "Quit blaming yourself. You're human. You did the best you could under some hellish circumstances. You're damn lucky those smugglers didn't start firing at you. Hell, you could have been killed too!"

His touch was excruciating, awakening her dormant senses to an agonizing awareness. What he said was true. She knew that in her head. But her heart—her heart was shattered with the loss of Dave. She had lost two men whom she had loved and cared for deeply in the span of a year. Dave had been like a replacement for her brother Cal, whom she adored but rarely saw anymore.

"Oh, Bram . . ." she whispered rawly, "I hurt so much inside for Dave's wife and his children . . ."

"Come here," he ordered sternly, and took her into his arms, crushing her against his body. He had felt her hesitate initially but then Storm had fallen against him like a supple willow. He groaned, feeling her softness yield against the hard planes of his body. He placed one hand against her silken hair, aware of her special female fragrance that thrilled all his senses. She buried her head on his shoulder, crying softly, and he held her, rocking her gently in the darkness, murmuring comforting words of solace near her ear.

Finally the tears eased and so did the pain she had been carrying in her heart. The feel of being held was overwhelmingly consoling to her ravaged spirit, and Storm nuzzled into Bram like a lost kitten beneath his solid jaw, content to remain there. Other senses were coming to life within her, though, as she became aware of his steady heartbeat, his male scent, and the strength of his arms around her body, providing her with safety. It was all so crazy. She had known Bram Gallagher less than a week, and here she was in his arms. Somehow it seemed right, and she knew he felt the same way.

Bram stroked her hair. "Better?" His voice was husky.

Storm nodded, not wanting to pull away but knowing she must. Reluctantly she placed her hands on his chest, looking up into his shadowed unreadable face. His cobalt eyes gleamed, sending a shiver of longing coursing through her.

"I'm sure you need this on top of everything else," she said, her voice hoarse.

A slight smile curved the corners of his mouth. "I don't consider you a problem, Storm." His arms tightened momentarily against her, and she became wildly aware of his arousal, her body tingling with an aching fire of its own. "Matter of fact, if you want the truth, it's nice to be needed again."

Her heart wrenched as she heard the pain reflected in his voice. He had tried to disguise it with lightness, but she had heard the inflection. Bram was affecting her sensually, and Storm fought to maintain a level of lucidity. Stepping out of his embrace, she said, "You don't need me crying on your shoulder."

Again that same smile warmed her heart. "How long has it been since you cried, Storm?"

Touching her flushed cheeks with her palms, she closed her eyes. "A year."

"I'm glad you decided to put those tears on my shoulder, then," he said, pointing to the darkened patch on his flight uniform.

She managed a partial smile. "Masochist."

"You got it. Come on; feel like walking back now?"

Storm hesitated, her eyes widening. "I-I'm afraid I'll wake them up again with my screams."

Bram shook his head. He slid his hand around her waist, pulling her against him and urging her to walk beside him. "It won't come back tonight, Storm."

She stared up at him in a daze. "Promise, Bram?" She felt the unreasonable fear of a little girl. And right now she needed his reassuring strength. He gazed down at her, pulling her close for just a second and then releasing her.

"I promise, princess," he whispered huskily.

At one thirty P.M. the next day, the pilots who would stand the next twenty-four hour alert relieved them. Storm welcomed the transition with bloodshot eyes. All she wanted to do was finish out her day at the office and then get home and relax in a hot tub of water. As Bram had promised, she had had no more nightmares.

But her sleep was light and broken. The next morning each of the pilots had come and talked individually with her, their concern evident. It almost made her cry again. Bram had remained in the background, watching her, their eyes occasionally meeting, but allowing the other men to show their concern toward her. It was this family feeling that had made Storm realize long ago that she would never give up this wonderful career. She gained a sense of achievement when they rescued people from life-threatening situations. And when she needed support, the pilots and crews were there for her—just as she had always been there in the past for each of them and their families.

Bram walked with her toward the parking lot. He glanced down at her. "Why don't you go home and get some rest," he suggested.

"I intend to." Storm gazed up at his strong, confident face. "What will you do this evening?"

He snorted. "Unpack. I just bought a house, and everything is still in boxes."

She frowned. He was alone, without family and friends here at a new duty station. And on top of that, just divorced. Storm remembered what it was like when Hal had died. If it hadn't been for the other pilots' families inviting her over for dinner or just coming to visit, she probably wouldn't have made it.

"W-would you like to come over for a home-cooked meal tonight?" she ventured.

Bram's brows shot up, his eyes mirroring surprise. It made her heart wrench when she realized just how human he was. Seeing usually the bulwark of strength surrounding him, it was easy for Storm to forget that he was a man with vulnerabilities, weaknesses, and strengths like anyone else. His boyish response stole her heart away.

"A home-cooked meal?"

She gave him a genuine smile, halting at her sports car. "Yeah. Real food. Nothing out of a can. Well?"

Bram grinned broadly, excitement shining in his blue eyes. "Sure."

Taking a pen from the pocket on the left arm of her flight suit, Storm dug out a small notepad from her pants pocket, scribbling down her address and phone number. "Here," she said, slipping the paper into his hand. "If you get lost, give me a call. I doubt you will. Opa-Locka is too small to get lost in. Or if you can't make it, call me."

He stared down at the paper and then up at her. There was a newfound gentleness in his expression. "You don't have to do this, Storm."

"You're right. I don't do anything I don't want to. See you at six thirty, Bram."

Bram arrived at exactly 1830. The door was open, and he peered through the screen as he knocked.

"Come on in," Storm called.

She dried her hands on a towel, meeting him as he wandered through the foyer on his way to the kitchen. A smile lit up her features when she saw him. He was dressed in a pair of well-worn jeans that hugged his lower body and a pale blue short-sleeve shirt. He smiled, handing her a bottle of wine.

"I didn't know if you were going to have fish or meat, so I compromised on a rosé," he said by way of explanation.

Storm was touched by his thoughtfulness, and she detected a hint of shyness in him. In Bram Gallagher? Maybe she had misread the man behind the brash Air-Force image. He was clean-shaven, his eyes clear and hair still damp from a recent shower. "Actually I thought barbecued chicken was in order. It's easy to fix, and we can stay outdoors until the mosquitoes decide to get their required pint of blood."

"Chicken sounds delicious," he responded with a smile.

"Come on. You can help me make the salad. I assume you eat vegetables?"

"Yeah, I like rabbit food."

Storm laughed, feeling high with happiness. She noticed the way he looked at her, and it sent the blood rushing to her cheeks. Once in the small kitchen, she gave him a cutting board, a knife, and some radishes.

"You cut those up, and I'll slice the green pepper."

Bram raised one eyebrow, casting a look over at her as she worked a few feet away. "Anyone ever suggest you wear shorts and a tank top to work instead of a flight suit?"

Storm shot him a look. "A few people," she admitted.

"I'll bet it was more than just a few," he rejoined, grinning. Damn, she had the most beautiful pair of legs he had seen in a long time. They were long, shapely, and golden-tanned. But more than that, there wasn't an ounce of fat on her. "You jog by any chance?"

"Religiously. And you?"

"Not so religiously. Maybe a couple miles every second or third day. You?"

Storm squelched a smile, her heart fluttering in her

breast. He was good for her badly deflated feminine ego. "Three miles a day whether I want to or not."

"I can tell," he murmured appreciatively. Not only that, but the light pink tank top clung to her like a second skin, revealing nicely rounded breasts.

"Thank you," she said, forcing herself to pay attention to the green pepper. Otherwise she'd end up cutting off her fingers, he affected her so strongly.

"You look better, Storm," he said, looking up from his duties.

"I climbed into a hot tub and soaked for a while. It does wonders, believe me."

"No more dark shadows under those beautiful gray eyes of yours."

"Flatterer."

"You need it."

"Being a chauvinist again?"

Bram grinned boldly. "Hardly. After I got over the initial shock that you were really a pilot, and, to top it off, my AC, I decided to change my attitude and enjoy the scenery."

Storm laughed, shaking her head. "One of these days, Gallagher, all that Irish blarney that comes so trippingly off your tongue is going to get you into trouble," she promised, walking by him. She hesitated at the door, catching the widening smile on his face. There was an incredible naturalness that existed between them no matter where they were. Bram was the first man she had invited into her cloistered existence since Hal's death. And she was glad it was him.

"Usually," he informed her archly, "this quicksilver tongue of mine gets me *out* of trouble, not into it."

"I hope you speak Spanish, then."

"I do. And German. And French. Satisfied?"

"I'm impressed. I can barely speak English fluently."

"Lady, all you have to do is just stand there. Your

eyes speak eloquently enough for you," he said throatily, catching her widening gaze.

Flustered, Storm had no quick answer. "When you finish, bring the salad and come join me outside."

Bram cocked his head. "What's the matter, the heat getting to be too much in the kitchen?"

"Wise guy," she taunted. "I'm going to open that bottle of wine. We can sit in the shade drinking it while the chicken gets done."

He grinned. "I'll see you in a few minutes."

The house was a one-story ivory stucco with wooden shutters that could be closed to protect the windows during hurricane season. As Bram wandered through it he decided that he liked the warmth of Storm's home. And it was a home, he decided, admiring the pale peach walls and burnt orange furniture coupled with brass and glass coffee tables and lamps. She had good taste, but then, that was obvious in her personal sense of style and quality.

The backyard was enclosed by a six-foot-high fence. A large cypress tree with hanging moss drooping off its limbs dominated the center of the yard. Storm was busy basting the succulent chicken in spicy sauce when he ambled out the back door with the bowl of salad in his hands. He ducked beneath the spreading arms of the cypress to join her. She had opened the bottle of wine and placed it on the picnic table, two glasses poured and waiting. Picking them up, Bram handed one to Storm when she had completed her duties.

"Let's toast," he said, touching her glass with his, gravely meeting her gray eyes. "To a friendship that will last a lifetime from this day onward."

Her lips parted and for a precious second, Storm lost all coherent thought as she met his midnight blue eyes that touched her aching heart and body. Swallowing, she nodded. "Yes, to friendship. The very best of all worlds combined," she murmured sincerely, taking a sip of the rosé.

Bram watched her intently as he drank. Her face was flushed from working over the barbecue. There was a luminous glow to her features that made her appear eighteen-years-old. Now her gray eyes were lively and not as somber as before. Wispy bangs had been dampened where they touched her brow, her ginger hair curving around her square face, lending her a softness he hadn't been aware of before. Or had he? Bram wanted to say out loud, Stop; don't say another word. Just stand there and let me drink in all of you, Storm. Let me map out your face in my mind's eye so I can carry it with me forever. . . . Whatever could he be thinking? Disgruntled with his own rampant thoughts, he sat down opposite her, appreciating her long thoroughbred legs.

"You acted surprised when I invited you over for dinner," Storm said, breaking into his thoughts.

Bram roused himself, meeting her curious gaze. "I didn't want you to do it because you felt you had to. Just because I held you and maybe helped you last night doesn't mean you owe me anything."

She warmed to his honesty. "That wasn't the reason, Bram."

"What was?"

"I tried to imagine what it would be like to move to a new base where you knew no one. You have no friends here"—she lowered her lashes—"and without a wife, I figured you had to be awfully lonely."

He took another sip of wine. In a way, he wished he had something stronger to drink right now to numb his mind and body, which were responding to Storm on a physical level. He had to fight himself. "So you felt sorry for me?"

"No. Compassion."

His blue eyes sparkled. "Thanks. I'm glad I'm not here out of pity."

"Pity is the most useless emotion in the world," Storm answered softly, her tone suddenly serious.

"That and guilt."

"Ouch. I'm afraid I'm still carrying around that particular emotion with me."

Bram slid his long strong fingers around the beaded coolness of the wineglass. "Because of Dave's death?"

Storm sobered. "Yes."

"About five years ago I lost my radar-navigator when we had to bail out of the Phantom I was flying," he told her in a softened voice. "Chuck had to go first because if I bailed out, the blast of the ejection could have injured him. Apparently his ejection seat wouldn't work, so he tried to manually bail out, but that didn't work either." He shrugged, resting his arms on his thighs and staring down at the grass. "I bailed out at seven-thousand feet in that dive figuring I'd die, too, because I'd passed all the altitude limits for safe ejection. I thought I'd end up eating dirt before my chute pack ever opened."

Storm grew solemn. "Thank God, you didn't die." The fervency of her hushed words startled them both. She blushed deeply, at a loss for words. She nervously fingered the stem of the wineglass, suddenly rising to busy herself with turning the chicken over on the grill.

Bram sat back, watching her. There was an indefinable magic simmering between them. He had felt it that first day in the hangar when they met. Despite his shock, he had been drawn to Storm. And last night, when she had cried in his arms, his closed, guarded heart had reached out to comfort her. Storm had been like a lost, frightened child in those precious twenty minutes, entrusting herself completely to his protection. And it had brought out a side of him that had rarely surfaced before. Storm was strong-willed, like himself;

nevertheless, she had not lost her vulnerability or her femininity. She had not lost the ability to lean on someone when she was weak. A smile played on his mouth as he watched her beneath half-closed eyes. You are rare, he told her in his thoughts. Just as rare as your name. . . .

"How did you end up with a name like Storm?" he asked suddenly.

Storm took a deep breath, thankful to be on safer ground with him. She sat back down, crossing her slim legs. "My mother loves thunderstorms, so, that's how I got the name," she explained. "I guess I howled lustily in the delivery room, and Mom put two and two together and came up with Storm."

He grinned with her. "It's a beautiful name."

"Growing up with it wasn't," she laughed. "It got me into more trouble. The kids all thought I was a scrapper of some sort. Cal and Matt, my brothers, ended up defending me a lot as a consequence."

"You're a lover, not a fighter," Bram interjected.

She shrugged bashfully. "I'll take the fifth on that one."

"Everyone thought you were a cloudburst just ready to rain on somebody's parade?"

"That was about the size of it."

"So tell me, how in the hell did you end up as a Coast Guard helicopter pilot? Was it your name?"

Storm laughed. "No, my father owns a crop-dusting business here in Florida. He uses helicopters instead of fixed-wing aircraft to spray the orchards. They live over in Clearwater, as a matter of fact. He's spent his life dusting orchards all over the state."

"So you were born with a cyclic in the right hand and a collective in the other," he teased.

"Almost." Her gray eyes grew warm with fond memories. "You have to meet my parents to appreciate them, Bram. My mother was a feminist long before the word was even coined. And my father was never one to put women under his foot or in their place. So when I came along, I started riding in helicopters like Cal did from age seven on. I soloed at age sixteen and flew with my father until I entered Coast Guard flight school. The rest is history—I've been in SAR ever since, one way or another. And I hope to stay in it another ten years before they move me up the chain of command to manning a desk instead.''

He rested his chin against his folded hands, enjoying her openness and warmth. ''I like the confidence you have in yourself,'' he declared. ''You have a career that complements your strengths.''

''And my weaknesses,'' she reminded him. ''I have my Achilles' heel too, Bram.''

''You going to tell me what they are, or do I have to find out for myself?'' he teased.

''I think it would be dangerous to tell you.'' She laughed.

Storm rose and brought over the blue and white china plates. The chicken was done. Ladling out two huge spoonfuls of potato salad onto his plate, she handed it to Bram. ''How many pieces of chicken?''

Bram came around the end of the table, standing next to her at the barbecue. ''Three?''

''Hungry, aren't you?'' she commented dryly.

''When it comes to home cooking, lady, I'll eat more than my fair share.''

Storm smiled, placing the chicken on his plate. She chose a breast for herself and joined him at the table. The tangy salt breeze moved the humid air just enough to make it pleasant beneath the enfolding arms of the huge old cypress tree. Bram dug into the meal as if he were starving and it touched her heart. A softened smile touched Storm's lips, but she said nothing.

4

After dinner, Storm brought out a fresh strawberry pie replete with whipped cream topping. She laughed as she cut Bram a piece, handing it to him.

"There's no secret in how a woman gets to you."

He grinned appreciatively. "What? Through my stomach?"

"Yes."

"Listen, after struggling through a year of my own cooking, you're probably right." He gave her an arch look. "Why? Are you trying to get my attention?"

Storm grinned merrily, cutting a piece of the pie. "Not at all, Lieutenant Gallagher. Besides, I wouldn't want a man to love me just for my cooking abilities."

He dawdled over the pie, watching her. "What would make you interested in a man?"

Casting a quick look over at him, Storm realized their teasing had turned serious and her heart beat unsteadily in response. She placed both elbows on the table, meeting his curious gaze. "I was married to a wonderful man for five years before he died in an accident, Bram." Her gray eyes darkened with pain. "We were the best of friends. We enjoyed each other's company whether it was sharing a mutual career or just doing housework together."

"So, friendship is important to you?"

She nodded, studying the pie and realizing her appetite had fled. "When we made our toast earlier, I meant what I said about friendship being the very best of all worlds combined." Storm gave him half a smile. "The bedroom scene is important, but lust dies very quickly compared to real love."

"But it can be fun while it's happening."

She grinned with him. "I suppose you're right—if that's all you expect out of it and realize it's not a very sturdy foundation for a relationship."

His blue eyes glimmered with mirth. "What else is important to you in a relationship, Storm?"

"Honesty."

Bram nodded soberly. "I'll drink to that." He paused for a moment. "I gather your husband was in the Coast Guard also?"

Storm took a deep breath. It was the first time she had ever discussed Hal's death. Yet here now with Bram, it seemed right, and she followed her intuition. "Yes. We met at my first assigned station, which was Air Station Clearwater. I was assigned to fly the larger helicopters, the twin-engine H-3Fs."

"So, you were his copilot?"

"Yes. During the following year, we fell in love. Spending so much time together as a crew, we discovered we had a lot in common."

Bram heard the wistful note in her voice and envied her. "I wish I could say my exploration into marriage was as good," he said harshly.

Storm tipped her head, giving him a look full of

compassion. "Interesting that you call it an exploration," she murmured.

He finished off the pie, then poured the last of the rosé into their wineglasses. "I was single until I was twenty-six, Storm."

"Wild oats to sow by any chance?"

"Probably. I was having too much fun living it up. Flying hard, meeting the boys regularly over at the Officers' Club afterward for drinks, and enjoying the women who liked to be in the company of fighter pilots."

Storm's eyes glimmered with laughter, and he saw it, giving her a rueful grin.

"Hey, life to me is one nonstop adventure. I don't apologize to anyone for what I did or didn't do. I took full responsibility for my actions. Sometimes I had a great time. Sometimes I crashed and burned."

"Can't you use some other metaphor?"

"Fighter jock talk, that's all," he assured her, smiling.

"So, one of these fast women finally settled her loop around you, and you got married?" Storm asked.

"Maggie had red hair, green eyes, and a temper to match," he told her. "I liked her spunk. There was always excitement wherever she went, and I wanted to be a part of it."

Storm rested her chin on her folded hands, curbing a knowing smile. "So, how long did it last?"

"Five years. And looking back on it, I was kind of proud of the fact that it held together that long." He looked up at Storm. "Maggie didn't like being tied down to one place too long. She said she had nomadic blood in her veins or some such thing. Blamed it on her need to travel and to be in a constant state of motion and animation."

"So, she didn't like being base-bound?" Storm asked, thinking that any woman who married a career officer had to get used to some less than wonderful conditions at air bases.

"You got it."

"Did you really love her, Bram?"

He ran his fingers through his hair. "Honestly? Yes. But it was that romantic lust you were talking about earlier that was the reason I married her. It was great for a year, but after that, things faded fast."

She stared at him intently for a moment. "From the tone in your voice, I'd say you loved her a great deal even though your reasons for getting together were different at first."

Bram refused to meet her knowing gray eyes. "How did you get to be so smart, Travis, and still be under thirty?" he growled.

"I can hear the pain in your voice, Bram. That's not age talking, it's wisdom."

He sat there, resting on his elbows, his face now placid and thoughtful. "I really did fall in love with Maggie during that first year," he admitted. "I liked her spirit, her zest for life." His voice dropped to a whisper and he shook his head. "The only trouble was, she didn't love me. She was happy for about a year, and then she more or less lost interest in married life. I hadn't. I saw the woman beneath her dazzling facade, and I fell in love with her."

Storm saw the anguish in his eyes when he talked of his ex-wife and reached out and touched his arm to give him solace. "Well, if it makes you feel any better, I've been emotionally crippled by this past year."

Bram smiled gently. "We're some combination, eh?"

Storm nodded thoughtfully. "I guess we've both lived through some hard times," she intoned. She grinned over at him. "Just a couple of sad cases, right?"

Bram raised one eyebrow and gave her that intent look that always thrilled her. "Well, with a pair like us, we have nowhere to go but up from here, right?"

"Right," Storm agreed. "If nothing else, we can make each other laugh when we're crawling around in our individual depressions."

Groaning, he got to his feet. "Don't remind me. I've been through enough hell this past year with Maggie leaving me and fighting my way through flight school."

"Well," she informed him dryly, "things will go better from here on out."

"Is that a promise?"

"Yup. Every dog has its day, Gallagher, and we'll have ours. We'll wind up winners; I promise."

Next morning Storm dressed in her light blue summer uniform to assume her duties as assistant training officer for the air station. Hooking the bright red and blue tie at her throat, she picked up her purse. The morning was beautiful, and she enjoyed driving to work with the top down on her sports car. All her thoughts centered on Bram and the wonderful dinner they had shared together. She liked the fact that Bram could poke fun at himself and admit the mistakes he had made. He was a man with tremendous confidence, but he didn't allow his ego or pride to get him into lasting trouble. That was a commendable trait, she thought. Just thinking about Bram's honest talk and easy laugh made her happy. He'd turned out to be even more special than she'd imagined. Smiling, she parked the car and walked into the Administration building.

Her office was located halfway down the passageway, on the left. LCDR Bob Moody was the training officer, and she was his assistant. Every pilot and copilot had collateral duties besides flying SAR. She grimaced, knowing the paperwork on her desk was going to be tremendous by today. The double load they all carried was awesome. There wasn't an officer around who didn't acknowledge the pressure of duty combined with a grueling SAR schedule. Taking off her cap as she walked into her office, Storm halted, her eyes widening. There, in the center of her neatly kept desk was one red rosebud in a beautiful cut-glass vase. The beginning of a smile touched her lips as she stared down at it in disbelief. Placing her purse and hat on the coat rack, Storm walked over to her desk and sat down, opening the card that was leaning up against the vase.

Dear Princess,
    Have lunch with me today at Pondi's Restaurant at 12:30. I'll buy.
                                Just another Sad Case

Storm smiled tenderly as she stared down at the scrawled handwriting. "Bram Gallagher, what am I going to do with you?" she whispered. Reaching out, she petted the velvety red bud, which was just beginning to unfold. It smelled heavenly. She sat back, shaking her head.

"Who's the secret admirer?" Bob Moody stuck his head into her office.

Storm smiled. "None of your business."

Bob grinned, leaning against the door jamb. "Well, whoever it is, it's about time, Stormie."

Laughing, she tucked the note into her desk. "You're as bad as Kyle and his gang. Trying to marry me off, Bob?"

"We just want to see you happy again, that's all," he reassured her.

Storm's heart ached with warmth toward him. "I know," she whispered, losing her smile. "And all you guys have been the best tonic in the world for me. You know that."

Bob rubbed his slender jaw, his brown eyes alight with enjoyment. "Yeah, but we're all married and can't chase after you ourselves. Whoever the guy is who sent you that rose had better appreciate what he has."

Storm pulled out some documents that were begging for her attention from the In file basket. "Oh, I think he does," she answered.

"Not going to tell me who, huh?"

"No."

"Lucky bastard," Bob said, smiling. "He'd just better damn well appreciate the fact that you're special, that's all."

Storm tried to quell her feelings of excitement throughout the morning. Every hour dragged by, and she had to force herself to stop watching the clock. My God, she was acting like an eighteen-year-old girl instead of a twenty-eight-year-old woman! Chastising herself, Storm concentrated on her given tasks, refusing to look at the clock anymore. But occasionally she did raise her head to stare dreamily over at the rose, inhaling the fragrant scent that hovered in her office like a delicate perfume.

Everyone else in Admin had left for lunch, so the place was practically deserted when Bram wandered through its doors. Dressed in dark blue slacks and the mandatory light blue shirt, he removed his garrison cap as he walked down the empty hall. He lightened his step as he neared her office and quietly came to a halt at the doorway in order to watch Storm work.

His eyes mellowed with warmth as he saw that she had placed the rose near her left arm, well within reach if she cared to touch or smell it. Out of the flight suit and in the more feminine apparel of her uniform skirt and blouse, Storm looked breathtaking in his eyes. Crossing his arms, he leaned up against the door, a grin playing at his lips as he watched her.

"Do you always work this hard?" he asked.

Storm jerked her head up with a gasp of surprise. Her heart leapt to a momentary thundering gallop. Closing her eyes, she placed her hand on her breast, leaning back in her chair.

"You scared the hell out of me, Bram!" she whispered.

"Sorry. Ready to eat?"

Laying down the pen, Storm smiled. "Sure am. I'm starved." Her face softened as she caressed the rose. "And thank you for this. It was a lovely surprise."

His smile was genuine. "Roses are always reserved for beautiful women."

She stood, coming around the desk and retrieving her hat and purse, a look of devilry in her gray eyes. "Is that more of the Gallagher malarkey designed to impress the woman he wants?"

Placing his hand beneath her elbow, he guided her out down the hall. "Absolutely." And then he gave her a wicked look. "Well, were you impressed?"

Laughing, she nodded. "Very. I love flowers, and it's been a long time since I've gotten some. It was a lovely thought, Bram," she whispered, becoming serious and meeting his midnight-blue eyes. "Thank you."

"No one ever said that two sad cases couldn't make each other smile every once in a while, did they?"

Storm smiled in agreement. "No, they didn't. And you certainly made my day, and then some. No matter what else goes wrong today, it won't faze me. All I have to do is touch that rose's velvet petals or lean over and smell its wonderful fragrance, and all my worries disappear."

Bram nodded, opening the door of his car for her. "You're a romantic at heart, Lieutenant Travis, and that appeals greatly to my instincts."

Storm paused, waiting for him to get in. When he did, she gave him a wicked look in return. "I just wonder which instincts you're referring to, Gallagher."

His glance was almost a leer. "You're just going to have to wait with bated breath to find out, aren't you?"

"You're impossible," she teased.

"Yeah, so I've been told."

Storm cringed inwardly when they entered Pondi's. It was a popular off-base restaurant located near the air station. Many of the pilots ate there as a change of pace from military cooking. Storm saw the looks on her friends' faces. What did they expect? Bram was her copilot! Still, the look on Kyle Armstrong's face and a few others' made her feel embarrassed. She was grateful for Bram's quick appraisal of the situation.

"Why do I get the feeling the rest of these fly boys are intensely protective of you and don't want to see you with another man?" he whispered near her ear.

"They mean well, Bram. They all knew Hal and you're seeing the family attitude at work," she explained lamely, sitting down opposite him in the booth. After ordering a drink and their lunch, Storm relaxed, enjoying Bram's presence. She decided to ignore the speculative looks they had received.

"We're scheduled for a training flight tomorrow morning," he informed her.

"Oh?"

"Yeah, I guess the Ops officer wants me to get my feet wet in a hurry. We have training scheduled every other day for the next month."

"I'm not surprised."

"Is it because I was a jet jockey at one time?" he asked wryly.

Storm shook her head. "No, it's because of hurricane season coming in late August through October, Bram. They don't want any pilot going out with a green copilot in weather situations that arise during that time of year. I imagine Commander Harrison figured you could take the punishment of the training to protect you and me."

"But that means that you're logging in a hell of a lot more time in the cockpit getting me trained."

"I can take it," she assured him, trying not to smile.

She liked his protectiveness toward her. "Are you always this protective?"

Bram shrugged, taking the Scotch and water that the waitress handed to him. "Maggie always accused me of being overprotective. She said it suffocated her. Maybe I am. Just part of my nature."

Lifting the vodka gimlet to her lips, Storm took a sip. Setting it back down, she said, "Well, I find it kind of refreshing."

"Aha, you mean you're not all feminist?" he challenged.

"I think I'm a nice blend of present with past," she defended herself archly. "I don't want any male to tell me what he thinks I can or cannot do. That should be left up to me to decide."

"But you still love flowers and will let a man take you to dinner?"

"You bet."

"Thank God!" Bram countered, raising his eyes heavenward.

Her laughter was full and unrestrained, and Storm didn't realize that the other pilots in the restaurant were smiling in response.

5

Storm, wake up!" Bram called, giving her shoulder a gentle shake. He heard her mumble incoherently, turning slowly on her back. Even in the shadowed darkness of the alert quarters, he could see the exhaustion in her features.

"What?" she asked thickly.

"We have a rescue," he explained, gripping her hand and helping her sit up. "Didn't you hear the alarm go off?"

"Uh," she groaned, rubbing her face tiredly. "No—I guess not . . . I'll be out in a second. Just let me get my boots on. . . ."

Bram waited in the silence of the lounge, watching her stumble out of the sleeping quarters. The last month and a half was beginning to tell on both of them, but particularly on Storm. He worried about the paleness of her features. "Come on," he coaxed, putting his hand on her elbow, "The ODO wants to see us right away."

They rode down to Ops in a companionable silence.

Lieutenant Kenny Hoffman glanced up as they entered the office.

"Grab a cup of coffee," he told them, pointing to the percolator.

"I'll get it," Bram told her.

Storm gave him a grateful look. "Thanks. Okay, Ken, what do we have?"

He shook his head woefully. "Figure it out—the weather deteriorates to fog so damn thick you can cut it with a knife, and everybody gets into trouble." He went over to the large map that hung on the back wall. "We received word earlier from Communications that a light plane ditched. The source of the call was unknown and came in on a VHF-FM radio."

She took the cup of coffee from Bram, thanking him silently with her eyes. Taking a sip, she sat it down, starting to scribble some necessary information on the briefing form that would be needed for the case. "Any FAA flights through that area?"

"Yeah, one. It appears to be the plane that ditched. It's only twenty miles offshore, so that will give you plenty of on-scene time in the area to try and find them."

"God only knows how in this fog," Bram murmured, gazing out the window at the thick gray curtain.

Ken nodded unhappily and peered over at Storm. "I have a Falcon crew who will be going up in about twenty minutes. They'll use their radar to home in on the ditched plane's debris, and they'll vector you in to where it's located. I've got a cutter on its way. If you can't locate the aircraft, they'll stop every few minutes and listen for people in the water near the crash area."

"Good," she muttered. "If we can't get down in the water to rescue them, then the cutter can get to them instead."

"You got it."

She looked at him, her eyes dark and troubled.

"How many people aboard that flight, or don't they know, Ken?"

The officer avoided her look, his mouth becoming a thin line. "It's a family, Storm."

She sucked in a deep breath, chewing on her lower lip. "Kids too?"

Kenny nodded. "Yeah, two. Parents, two kids, and grandparents, unfortunately."

"Dammit," she whispered rawly, casting a glance up at Bram. Somehow his solid breadth assuaged her. In the past month and a half, they had become an inseparable team, learning to rely on each other during several life and death situations. Bram could be trusted completely, and right now all she wanted to do was lean against him and rest. But rest had evaded them. All they had done was fly, train, and work at their respective desk jobs. There had been little time for personal contact. She saw Bram's blue eyes dim as he held her gaze. He knew she was close to exhaustion.

"I'll get with Merlin on our helo," he said.

"I'll be out as soon as possible," she promised.

Storm was settling the helmet on her head when Bram climbed aboard. He gave Merlin a pat on his thin shoulder by way of greeting and made his way forward into the shaded cockpit. The luminescent red glow from the instrument panel cast eerie shadows across their faces as they worked in unison, strapping into their harness system and going through the necessary instrument checks. Bram brought the microphone close to his mouth, glancing over at Storm.

"You know the Air Force has a good term we ought to use," he said lightly. "All the SAC bomber crews use it."

She tiredly turned her head. "What's that?"

"Ready, ready now."

A slight smile pulled at her lips. "Are we?"

"Sure. Want me to take navigation?"

Flying was the easier of the two. "I'd appreciate it, Bram."

"You got it, princess. Ready, ready now."

She warmed to the nickname he had christened her with that night out on the ramp when she had cried in his arms. Occasionally he would stroke her with the intimate phrase, and it never ceased to lift her failing spirits.

"Flatterer," she accused.

His grin broadened in the darkness, teeth starkly white against his shadowed features. "Until my dying day."

"Dying isn't funny, Bram."

"Come on, Storm, chin up. It was a joke."

After getting clearance for takeoff, Storm listened to the engine's whine increase as she pulled the 52 up into the murky whiteness of the fog. At thirty-five-hundred feet, they climbed far above the white blanket that stretched as far as they could see. Above the fog, the night was clear. It was a beautiful sight as the starlight struck the surface of the fog below them. Merlin busied himself with assembling the items that might be needed for the rescue in case they found the ditched plane before they began the track over the ocean.

"Hey, we get a day off tomorrow," Bram reminded her.

"It's a good thing. I'm going to spend it sleeping," Storm said wearily.

"How about after you wake up? Got any plans for the rest of it?"

She scowled. "Oh, just a week's worth of laundry, the house desperately needs a cleaning, and—"

"Come to the beach with me, Storm. We need time away from everything." He looked over at her, his eyes searching her features. Her skin had an opalescent glow to it, the flesh pulled tightly across her cheekbones, accenting her fatigue. "I'll bring the picnic basket and pick you up at three."

"But we don't even get off until one thirty," she protested. And then she glanced at her watch. "It's almost 0500 now."

"Trying to tell me no?"

"No." She grinned. "It sounds great, Bram, but I'm afraid I won't be much company. I'm beat."

"I'm not asking you along to entertain me, Storm," he returned dryly. "Let me take care of the details and do the worrying for both of us, okay? Just give me an unqualified yes or no."

She smiled softly. "Yes."

"Good."

"Don't gloat about it."

"Was I?"

"You know you were, Bram, so quit playing coy with me."

His laughter filled her earphones, and she grinned at him. She loved his irrepressible spirit. There had been times in the recent past when she had been grouchy and just plain irritable. But he had taken it in easy stride, cajoling her with teasing to bring her back to a better frame of mind. "I don't want to be a killjoy about this, but with the fog as bad as it is, I doubt it'll burn off in time for the beach."

"Killjoy."

"Sorry. Just giving you the facts."

"Where's that romantic streak in you, Travis? You know the sun's going to shine for us when we go to the beach."

She gave him a long look. "I might be a romantic but you're a confirmed idealist, Gallagher."

"And you love me for it. Don't you?"

Shaking her head, Storm muttered, "I give up on you."

"No, you don't. I haven't met a woman yet who didn't like a man who challenged her. And you're no exception to that rule."

Their banter provided much-needed relief, and no one appreciated it more than Storm. Bram always had the ability to lighten the atmosphere when things got tense. Well, she thought grimly, it was really going to be tense when they sank back into the fog to fly the mandatory track that would hopefully lead them to where the plane had ditched. Merlin would have to watch for a sign of flares from the ocean—that is, if there were any survivors, and if they were in the area pinpointed by the Coast Guard.

"Better go down," Bram told her. "We're over the track."

"Roger. Merlin, you got your eyes peeled?"

"Sure do, lieutenant."

Compressing her lips, she put the helicopter into a gradual descent, sinking down into the cottony thickness of the fog. Within seconds, they were flying through total whiteness. All her concentration zeroed in on the helicopter instruments. She took the 52 down to a hundred-and-fifty feet off the water's surface. With the fog this heavy, no one would be able to spot a flare or any other kind of light at a higher altitude. If a flare was to be spotted at all . . .

Bram read the altitude to her every few minutes. She held the helicopter steady, thankful that there was barely any wind and the ocean was calm.

They continued their radio and flare search for the survivors. The Falcon jet high above them got a contact on radar. Bram glanced over at her.

"What do you want to do?"

"We'll drop to fifty feet at thirty-five knots of air speed over the area they've pinpointed. Read off the altitude as I descend."

"Roger. Seventy-five feet . . . seventy . . ." He continued to call out the altitude until she hit fifty. "Keep her steady at fifty. Want me to fly some?"

"Not yet." Her eyes ached from the strain of watching the instruments. It was too easy to get disoriented in fog and lose one's sense of direction. Bram knew how to fly on instruments but had little experience flying in this kind of weather. Storm would have to keep flying despite her fatigue.

They worked a track pattern crisscrossing the unseen ocean below them for almost fifteen minutes. Bram had the navigation chart spread across his thighs, calling off coordinates when they had to make another turn and take in a new unexplored part of their search pattern. Somewhere up above them, dawn was occurring, she thought. If only they had some light—anything would help. Glancing at the fuel gauge, they had another twenty minutes before they'd have to go back to base to refuel. It was 0600. The tension was palpable in the cabin; each of them was fully aware of the danger of flying so close to the ocean's surface. One slight move and they could be buying into a chunk of watery real estate.

"Target at four o'clock at twenty yards!" Merlin cried triumphantly. "A red flare!"

"Drop a Datum Marker Buoy," Storm ordered. "We always drop a DMB or a float flare so we can vector back to it, Bram," she explained.

Merlin tossed the DMB out the door seconds after her initial command.

Bram looked out the right window at her right shoulder. "Circle to the right, Storm," he ordered.

She brought the 52 around heading back toward the spot. Their eyes narrowed as they slowly passed over the area again. Storm's hands rested tensely on the controls as Bram tried to probe the fog.

"Why didn't we just fly toward the target Merlin saw?" he asked.

"Because we don't know what the Falcon saw on radar, Bram. Also, Merlin saw a flare. It could be from a sailing ship in distress. If we get in too big of a hurry and are not careful circling back to the object, we just might crash into a ship's mast or something."

He grinned tightly. "I see your point."

"That's right." Storm frowned. "Sure you didn't see spots before your eyes, Merlin?" she asked.

"Swear to God I didn't. I saw the red flicker of a flare. I know I did."

"I hope he did," Bram said.

"Yeah. I'm coming back to the left, Bram. Maybe we should have gone left in the first place."

"Ten lashes with a wet noodle."

She shook her head, a tired smile edging her mouth. "Sorry, I'm no masochist. You are, remember?"

"Oh, yeah, I forgot. Want to play the role of the sadist?"

Storm chuckled as Bram continued to look out the cockpit window. "No, thank you. I like myself just the way I am."

"That makes two of us."

"You're such a—"

"There!" Merlin cried.

Storm saw the feeble glare of a red flare staining the fog. "Merlin may need your help at the door once we set down," she told Bram.

"Right."

Circling the inverted light aircraft, the wash of the rotor blades made the fog swirl and twist into strange patterns as they approached.

"I count four people," Bram said. He called in the necessary information back to the base.

Merlin was busy in the back, getting prepared to slide open the door once they landed.

"Okay," Storm muttered, bringing the 52 into a hover. She studied the ocean surface. It consisted of long rolling swells with no waves. Perfect for landing, Storm thought, breathing a sigh of relief. For once, something was with them instead of against them.

"Bram, tell base to stand by in case we need medical assistance."

"Roger."

The next few moments the 52 hovered above the greenish ocean. The wash of the rotor blades spewed up froths of seawater around the survivors clinging weakly to the wreckage of the plane. Storm landed quickly and manipulated the controls to maneuver the helicopter closer so that the door could be opened directly toward the plane.

Merlin slid the door back and locked it into position, then lowered the rescue platform. He looked toward the cockpit.

"Lieutenant Gallagher, I think I could use your help."

"You got it." He glanced over at Storm and winked. "I'll be careful," he told her, seeing the sudden pang of anguish on her face.

"Do. There's only one gunner's belt. For God's sake, don't slip off that grating platform and fall into the ocean."

He grinned, then released the shoulder straps, and carefully extricated himself from the seat. He placed a hand on her shoulder and gave it a squeeze. "You aren't going to lose me," he soothed huskily. Then he was gone.

The rescue took almost twenty minutes. Worriedly Storm watched as the four survivors were brought aboard. The elderly woman fainted once she was safely in the helicopter. The older gentleman was in shock, cradling his wife in his arms. The little boy of six valiantly let go of the plane and swam the short distance so that Merlin could retrieve him from the warm water. Bram had to slip off the grate and rescue the little four-year-old girl who refused to leave the fuselage of the aircraft. Storm watched in silence as he swam the twenty feet, his white helmet with red reflecting tape visible on the dark ocean's surface. Her heart beat frantically in her breast while she watched him disappear into the plane. She knew he was capable, but her fear of losing another copilot only increased her anxiety.

Twisting a look over her shoulder, Storm watched as they got the four survivors huddled into the warming folds of blankets. All were in shock to some degree. Then Merlin locked the door, and Bram clamored forward, soaking-wet. His face was dripping with water as he lowered himself into the seat, strapping back in.

"That's it," he said, removing his flight gloves and dropping them on the deck behind him.

"What about the others? Ken had said six were on board the plane."

"Both parents are dead. I checked them over—no pulse. Both bodies are trapped in the cockpit. When the cutter arrives, they can retrieve them."

Her lips thinned. "You positive?" They never left a rescue until everyone was accounted for.

"I'm afraid there's no question. Looks like they lost consciousness on impact. The old man said they tried to revive them, but it was no go." He cast a glance back toward the hold of the ship. "The rest are all suffering from exposure and shock." He gave her a warming look. "I think Merlin could use my help back there as soon as we lift off," he said huskily. "The grandmother fainted, and the old gentleman isn't in any better shape." The sound of children crying forlornly filled the rear of the helicopter.

Storm nodded. "Okay." She applied power, and the 52 strained skyward, swallowed up into the fog once again. Climbing to fifteen-hundred feet, they broke free, the sunlight almost blinding them. Bram's hand wrapped around her arm, and he squeezed it gently.

"You look pale," he observed.

"I was scared."

"I know. I'm sorry, but the little girl wouldn't come. You saw how she clung to the wreckage."

Storm blinked back the tears. "Yes, I know. Look, go back and see if you can help."

"The kids just need to be held, I think."

"Okay."

"Hey . . ."

She looked up after he unstrapped, meeting his melting blue gaze. "What?"

A slight smile crossed his strong sensual mouth. "You're one hell of a woman, you know that?"

A shiver of expectancy raced through her, and she avoided his gaze. Bram eased himself out of the seat, making his way back into the hold of the helo.

The sun was weakly filtering through the layers of fog by the time they arrived at the base around 0700. The ambulance was standing by. The little girl clung mutely to Bram, her arms wrapped tightly around his neck and her face buried beneath his chin. The boy gripped Bram's hand fiercely as Merlin tried to urge him to get up from the seat and walk toward the open arms of the waiting paramedic standing outside the helicopter. Storm came back to the rear and helped Bram out of the helicopter with his two frightened charges.

Storm crouched down on the runway next to Bram to meet the children's frightened looks. The little girl sobbed, throwing herself into her embrace, her small arms wrapped awkwardly around her. Tears streamed down Storm's cheeks as she spoke soothingly to the child. Bram gently guided the boy into her arms and then he and Merlin helped the grandparents down from the helicopter, escorting them to the ambulance. The next ten minutes tore Storm's heart apart. Each of the children eventually left her arms and were taken by the paramedics and placed with their exhausted grandparents. She stood up, a feeling of helplessness over-whelming her as the doors to the ambulance closed.

Bram walked over. Just his nearness allowed all the tension to drain from within her. They were left alone, both standing beside the helicopter.

"Come on," he urged softly. "Let's get over to the line shack and finish the debriefing and then we can go home."

Her gray eyes were wet with tears as she looked up into his strong face and tender gaze. "Home? Do you know how good that sounds?"

He nodded, wanting to reach out and envelop her in a hug. Under the circumstances, it wouldn't have been correct military bearing. He quelled the urge, giving her a squeeze instead. "Come on. You've done enough for one day," he murmured.

The debriefing form blurred before her eyes. Storm forced her fragmented thoughts to fill it out accurately. She felt numb with fatigue and sadness. Ken questioned them at length until finally, by 0830, they were over at the Q, getting cleaned up and ready for their collateral duty. If another SAR case came in, they could again be called to fly. Luckily, however, there was only one case, and the other crews were called to fly it. By the time 1330 came and they were officially relieved of duty, Storm was groggy with exhaustion.

Slats of sun filtered through the gray overcast sky that hung stubbornly two-hundred feet above the air station. Bram walked silently at her shoulder, checking his stride for her sake. Storm waged an inner war, trying to deal with a gamut of emotions. She tried to forget about the two children who had clung to her for comfort after being rescued. She felt Bram's hand on her arm, and she slowly halted and looked up into his face.

"You're not even walking a straight line, Storm," he said, frowning.

"I'm drunk with fatigue," she admitted, not even bothering to try to smile.

One corner of his mouth lifted. "At least you'd pass the Breathalyzer test if the cops stopped you."

She felt the ache of tears in her throat. Bram's concern unleashed the wall of emotion she had been fighting to keep contained. "Please, let me go, Bram," she begged rawly. "Just let me go home. I need to sleep this off."

He looked at her gravely, his eyes concerned. "I'm taking you home. And no argument, Storm. You're in no shape to drive. Having to fly on instruments, combined with two SARs, has done you in."

Miffed, she pulled from his grip, anger tingeing her voice. "Dammit, I just flew on instruments for a couple of hours! I think I can negotiate a twenty-minute drive to my house."

Ignoring her, he gripped her arm and led her to his car, opening the door. "Get in," he ordered tersely, brooking no argument.

She didn't have the strength to protest. Glaring at him, she slid into the car, taking off the baseball cap and stuffing it in the side pocket of the flight suit. Once he was in the car she said in a weary voice, "I just want to be left alone, Bram. Is that too simple for you to understand?"

He rested his arms on the steering wheel, looking over at her. Shadows of exhaustion were beneath his eyes; the shading of his day-old beard made him appear more gaunt. He grimaced slightly as if experiencing momentary pain. "I'm doing this for your own good," he said heavily. "Hell, you couldn't even write one sentence in there this morning without making spelling errors. That isn't like you, Storm."

She felt the backlog of tears building and leaned against the car seat, shutting her eyes tightly. Storm didn't want him to see her cry, and she was angry at him. It was helpless anger, because Bram knew what was needed under the circumstances and she was fighting it. Why? she asked herself. The weight in her chest grew heavier. She felt his hand on hers, gripping it firmly, giving it a squeeze.

"What does the SAR manual say about survivors needing to talk after they're rescued?" he asked, his voice a low vibrating tone. "If you allow survivors to talk about the loved ones they lost, it will speed recovery?"

Tears streamed down her cheeks and tangled in her hair. Storm finally raised her head, turning to look at Bram. "I didn't want you to see me like this," she quavered hoarsely.

His hand tightened on her fingers. "Why? Did you think I'd respect you less?" A slight smile filled with tenderness curved his mouth. "So what if you're a pushover for the children? All of us were equally affected by them, Storm. I looked up once and saw tears in Merlin's eyes."

She bowed her head, her lower lip trembling as tears washed down her face. "I hate missions that involve children, Bram." She said it with such force and agony that she heard Bram groan softly.

"Come here, princess," he coaxed gently, taking her into his arms. "Come here and let it go . . ."

It was so easy to turn and bury her face in the folds of his flight suit and weep. Bram rocked her gently, stroking her hair, whispering soothingly as she released the flood of pent-up anguish for the now-orphaned children. The solid beat of his heart finally brought some semblance of steadiness back to her disordered state as she lay quietly in his arms afterward.

"The children always suffer the most," she whispered, barely opening her eyes. "The adults can take shock better; take the grief. But the children have no defense against it, Bram. No defense . . ."

"This is the part of SAR no one gets used to," he agreed faintly.

Slowly Storm pulled away, peering up into his suffering face. He was no less affected by it than she or Merlin. His blue eyes were suspiciously bright, and her heart contracted with a new emotion. A broken smile fled across her tear-stained lips. "I'm glad you're here, Bram."

He leaned down, placing a warming kiss on her lips, parting them, and taking her tears away. His eyes were a turbulent, stormy blue as he drew away, his hand caressing her cheek.

"I'm finding life's opened up a whole new chapter to me, Storm," he admitted thickly. "Part of it is the Coast Guard. But you're responsible for the rest." His eyes were tender with concern. "Let's get you home."

Storm awoke sometime around five that day, still feeling exhausted. Jogging three miles, then taking a hot shower helped clear her head. Inwardly she felt as if somehow she had been emotionally purged, leaving her empty inside. But that sort of numbness always followed a particularly harrowing SAR mission. Running her fingers through her damp hair, she thought of Bram's tender comforting, and she began to feel some of the depression lighten and evaporate.

The phone rang, interrupting her thoughts. Sitting down on the edge of the bed, Storm answered it.

"Hello?"

"Well, did you survive?"

She smiled, closing her eyes, loving the husky tone of Bram's voice. "Partly."

"I tried calling earlier, but you were out."

"I got up at five and went for a run. Figured it was the best way to throw off the depression."

"I could think of better ways to cheer you up," he suggested.

Storm laughed softly. "Will you ever change?"

"No, but I'm working on changing you."

A smile lingered on her lips. "I'm a lost cause, and you know it."

"I never take no for an answer. Hey, how about that picnic?"

"Now? It's almost—"

"Why not roast hot dogs and marshmallows tonight along the shore? Who said we had to go during the day?"

Her brows rose. "Say, that sounds nice. That way there aren't the tourists milling around."

"Yes, ma'am. It also means some privacy, and we can watch the moon rise together. Game?"

A new thread of excitement coursed through her. Suddenly Storm felt as if someone had lifted a hundred pounds from her shoulders. "It sounds wonderful, Bram," she agreed fervently.

"Just what the doctor ordered."

Laughing, Storm said, "Do you ever lose that undeniable sense of humor, Bram?"

"Never. When we quit laughing at ourselves in a bad situation, then the going *really* gets rough."

"I'm all for laughing, then."

"We'll drown our sorrows in a good bottle of wine tonight, trade a few stories around the campfire, and generally relax. How does that sound, princess?"

Storm cradled the receiver to her cheek, closing her eyes. She ached to have time alone with Bram. "You're a good salesperson. I'm sold."

He chuckled. "My mother always did say I could sell ice cubes to Eskimos."

The sun was sinking into the depths of the glasslike ocean as Bram made their campfire. The air was drier than usual, and Storm loved it. She breathed in the warm salty air and spread a well-worn blanket onto the sand nearby. The beach was devoid of human beings, most of them having been sunburnt during the day and retiring to their hotels to nurse their wounds. She sat back, hands resting on her long thighs, watching Bram. He wore a pair of threadbare jeans, almost washed free of their color, and a red T-shirt that outlined his magnificent shoulders and chest. A smile lingered in her eyes—he was beautiful to watch.

As if sensing her stare, he lifted his head. A few unruly strands of dark hair dipped on his brow as he smiled across the fire at her. "You look a-hundred-percent better than this morning," he told her, throwing a few more pieces of dried driftwood onto the licking flames.

"I can say the same for you."

"I guess that means we're a mutual admiration society," he teased, grinning boyishly.

Storm began to unpack the hamper, pulling out the chilled bottle of white wine and two plastic cups. "Must be. After all, if we don't love ourselves first, how can we possibly love others?"

Bram joined her, flopping down on his back and then rolling onto his side, propping himself up on one arm. He arranged the cups, waiting for her to pop the cork on the wine. "You know, that's one of the secrets to life," he said seriously.

"What? Loving ourselves first?"

"Yes. If you can't be content with yourself, forgive yourself, and in general accept yourself as you are, how can you do the same for others?"

Storm smiled distantly, pouring the wine. "Some people might accuse you of being selfish, Bram."

He raised the cup. "Let them." He raised his eyes, meeting hers. "Here's to love of self so that we have the capacity to love others . . ."

She gave him a guarded look and hesitantly clinked her cup against his, tasting the dry fruity wine. Bram looked supremely contented as he sipped his wine, watching the sun set in a rainbow palette of colors, and occasionally glancing over at her. It was a pleasant half-hour as they sat near each other on the blanket watching the light fade, allowing the silence between them to speak volumes.

A pale lavender stained the horizon, the darkness of night on its heels as Bram broke the silence.

"Why do you apologize for being human, Storm?" he posed softly, startling her with the question.

She stretched out next to him, resting her head in the crook of her arm. The question had been asked gently and without blame. "Explain," she said huskily, feeling the wine steal through her, making her utterly relaxed.

Bram poured the last of the wine into their cups, setting the bottle into the sand beyond the blanket. "This morning," he said. "I've been working with you for three months now, and you always get uptight when children are involved. Why are you so afraid to cry in front of me and not the other pilots?"

She rolled onto her stomach, frowning. "I'm afraid you'll think I'm weak. You never see the guys cry when there's been a bad SAR mission. They've gotten used to me doing it around them."

He snorted softly. "They cry in the arms of their wives when they get home."

Her gray eyes squinted as she recalled the times Hal had held her after highly emotional SAR cases. "Why are you asking me about crying, Bram?"

"Because I happen to think you're a highly sensitive individual who needs to let out what she feels," he explained quietly. "I've watched you bottle up a lot since we started working together."

"I can't sit in the cockpit bawling like a baby when I have to function, Bram."

"I know that."

"Then, what do you want from me?"

He placed the cup on the sand, pulling her next to

him, fitting her beside his male body. His cobalt eyes were flecked with gold as he searched her grave, pensive face. He traced the line of her brow, from cheek to square jaw with his fingers. "You," he whispered thickly. "I want to experience the full emotional range of Storm Travis. You share parts and pieces of yourself with me, but not all of you. I've stood by for three months watching, sensing, and feeling the woman who climbs into that flight suit and flies SAR. When things are tense, your voice is always calm. Always soothing. You make us all rally around you because we know you care. We know you know your job." A glint registered in his serious look as he caressed her satin cheek. "I've sat in that left seat watching you control that other half of you. I've seen you compress those beautiful lips into a thin line, controlling your emotions. I've watched your wide gray eyes go narrow with pain and anxiety. And I've seen you come off a mission and suppress it all." He stroked her hair, combing his fingers through the silken tresses. "And I've stood there wondering what or how you deal with all that you've seen."

Storm trembled beneath his tender touch. His fingers were sure, confident, stoking the fires of her dormant body into brilliant, yearning life. Bram was so overwhelmingly male that an ache spread outward from the lower region of her body. She had been wishing for this moment for over a month now. Yet Bram had never made a move to touch her or hold her again after that first night. It was as if he sensed her need to be approached slowly; he seemed to want to prove to her that his intentions were honorable and not selfishly based. As she stared up into his darkened face, highlighted by the flickering firelight, she knew that he was serious where she was concerned. Despite his joking and teasing, he wasn't the ex–fighter jock out on the make for a one-night stand. No, her instincts had told her from that very first night that he was a man of integrity. Hesitantly she pulled her mind back to focus on his question, her gray eyes widening with vulnerability.

"I don't do anything with it," she admitted slowly.

"Why?"

She gave a painful shrug, laying her head in the crook of his arm. "When Hal was alive, I could talk with him about it, cry on his shoulder . . ."

Bram took a deep breath. He reached down and gently cupped her face in his hands. "Do you know that I see every emotion register on your face, Storm?"

She gave a shake of her head. "No. If you do, you're the first to tell me that."

A corner of his mouth curved upward, and he leaned down, kissing her temple. She smelled of apricots, and the scent increased his need of her. "You speak with your eyes, Storm. Sometimes I see reflections of pain there, sometimes a wistful look, and . . ." he placed his finger beneath her chin, raising her lips to his mouth, ". . . sometimes longing . . ."

She felt his mouth tremble slightly as it grazed her lips. The featherlike touch incited a string of explosions along her nerve endings and instinctively, she slid her hand upward, caressing his neck and curling her fingers into his dark hair. His male scent was like an aphrodisiac, spurring her hungrily forward to meet his questing mouth. Her lips parted beneath his exploration. His breath was moist against her flesh, and she pressed her body forward, needing further contact with him.

Bram groaned, pulling her possessively against him, his hands on her hips, making her aware of his arousal. Her mouth opened, trusting him, asking him to drink of her honeylike depths. A pounding hunger throbbed through him, and the smoldering spark between them caught and exploded violently to life. Her returning hunger seared him; made him tremble with need of her. All of her. A delicious sense of joy spiraled between them as he unbuttoned her blouse, sliding his hand down across her taut, expectant breast. He felt her stiffen, arching unconsciously to him as his fingertips grazed the hardened peak of her nipple. Part of him wanted to hurry, but another part gloried in the moment with Storm. Never in his life had he wanted to take the time as now to love a woman totally, love her completely. Every cell in his body screamed out for want of Storm. He bent down with agonizing slowness after pulling the lacy bra away to capture the nipple; he wanted her to enjoy the time spent in each other's arms thoroughly.

A gasp escaped her tremulous lips as his mouth settled firmly on her breast, his teeth gently tugging at the nipple, sending frenzied nerve-tingling messages to her wildly aching lower body. Her fingers sank deeply into his shoulder muscles, and Storm cried out his name, begging him, needing him. Each calloused touch of his fingers on her body as he slowly undressed her was a tormenting brand. Her mind was banished, and only her heart dominated, pounding hard with every quickened breath she took. His lips scorched her body, teasing her mercilessly, and a moan of utter necessity clawed deep within her throat as she pleaded with Bram to take her higher and higher where there was only loving, giving, and taking. She felt his well-muscled body settle above her, his knee gently urging her thighs apart, and she opened her gray eyes, meeting, melting, beneath his fiery gaze tendered with love.

In that instant, Storm knew she loved him as she had never thought she could love another man. Bram was her match, her equal. He met her fearlessly on her own ground, coaxed her beyond it, and urged her to new heights of euphoria in every sense of the word. His hand slid beneath her hips and instinctively she arched upward, desiring oneness with him. She was unprepared for the jolting charge of pleasure, coupled with exhilaration, as he thrust deeply into her, branding her, making her his forever. Her lips parted, a sigh of absolute joy escaping her as she closed her eyes, bringing her arms up, pulling him down upon her to share the volcanic needs they brought to each other. Higher and higher the throbbing, fusing sensation of his body carried her until she felt like dissolving in rapture. The shattering climax made her freeze, and he held her tightly, increasing the pleasure, extending it for her, until she nearly fainted with fulfillment. Seconds later, when she felt his body tense, his husky voice murmuring her name, she held him close, wanting to hold him forever.

6

Cold?" Bram asked hoarsely, pulling her closer into his arms.

Storm shook her head, kissing his jaw, and tasting the salt of perspiration upon his flesh. "No, just deliriously happy," she murmured, resting weakly against his supporting shoulder.

He smiled, lying above her, his arm protectively thrown across her slender waist. The moon was barely edging the horizon, sending a thin stream of light across the quiet ocean. Only the breakers crashing into a foamy existence upon the sand disturbed the silent world around them. Bram drank in her relaxed face. A slight upward curve of her lips told him how she felt. Words weren't necessary. Running his fingers lightly across her golden skin, he smoothed away the dampness created by their loving.

"When they made you, they must have broken the mold," he told her quietly, marveling at the beauty of her tall athletic body.

Storm barely opened her eyes, relishing the sensations still simmering within her body. A lazy smile touched her lips. "Is that a compliment or an insult?"

Bram grinned. "You'll never hear me run you down, princess. It was a compliment. God, you have the most beautiful legs I've ever seen on a woman." And then a distressed expression came to his face.

"What's wrong?" Storm asked, concerned.

A silly grin spread across his mouth. "Oh, I was just thinking what a crying shame it is that you have to wear those damn baggy flight suits. They hide some nice features about you, lady."

Storm slid her hand upward, marveling at the strength of his arm and shoulder. "You know what I first thought when I saw you?" she asked wistfully, her voice barely above a whisper.

"Besides my being the epitome of an arrogant, sexist bastard at the time, you mean?" he asked, leaning over, brushing the full lips that were begging to be kissed again.

"Mmm," Storm murmured, savoring his strong mouth against hers. She reveled in his ability to excite her with the slightest touch.

Bram drew a half-inch away, his blue eyes alight with tenderness. "You're easy to please, you know that?"

"That's because you know what you're doing," she murmured huskily, opening her eyes to gaze at him. "Do you want to know what else I thought?"

He nodded. "Yeah. We got sidetracked," he said ruefully, "but I'm not apologizing."

She pressed herself to him and snuggled beneath his chin. "I thought you had the broadest set of shoulders I had ever seen. I thought you could carry the weight of the world around on them."

Bram grimaced. "They should have looked short, stubby, and deflated the day I met you, then. I was just coming out of one year of my life that had been a living hell. I didn't feel very strong or broad-shouldered, believe me."

Storm sobered, hearing the pain in his voice. She quickly embraced him. "It's a good thing our physical bodies don't resemble our emotional states, then." She chuckled. "Or else I would have looked like a blob of Jell-O out there at the helicopter this morning."

He nuzzled her, placing playful nibbling kisses along the clean line of her jaw to her delicate ear. "That's why we can be a couple of sad cases, and no one can tell the difference," he said, his breath sending waves of warmth across her slender neck.

Gently she pulled away, searching his eyes. "I don't think we need to refer to ourselves that way anymore, do you?"

Bram slowly sat up, bringing her back into his arms. "No, we don't. You've survived Hal's death, and I've discovered that I'm not the least bit sad."

Storm rested her cheek against his naked chest, the small fine hairs covering it tickling her. "Somehow, Bram," she whispered, "you've helped me rescue myself from my own personal tailspin." Tracing her fingers lightly across his collarbone, she closed her eyes, loving him. "I was so lost without Hal. It was as if half of me had been destroyed in that car accident. I was lonely . . ."

He kissed her hair. "You're a woman who's used to sharing all of herself with her mate, princess. And that's a very rare quality most men would kill for."

She laughed. "Bram!"

He smiled down at her, his eyes telling her he was very serious about his last statement. The smile died on her lips as she looked up at him like a wide-eyed child. He kissed her nose.

"You think I'm kidding?"

"No . . ."

His face grew somber. "The women I've known

aren't into sharing any more of themselves than necessary, Storm. Like I said before, they play a game. I'll
give this part of myself if you'll give me this." He
frowned. "Or they'll blackmail you with their bodies or
their emotions."

"And Maggie was like that?"

He nodded. "I don't blame her for it. I understood it.
I saw the psychological reasoning behind it. But it
wasn't what I wanted or expected. I thought that once
we got married, Maggie would begin to trust me with
herself. All of herself." He looked out toward the
blackened sea. "But I was wrong. She just went on
playing her childish emotional games to keep me in line,
so to speak."

Storm shivered, the dampness from the ocean beginning to creep inland. Bram gave her a concerned look
and reached over, retrieving her blouse and helping her
slide it back on. As they dressed she stole a look over at
him. He looked virile and irresistible in only a pair of
jeans, his chest deep and heavily muscled in the
dancing firelight. She turned, sliding her arms about his
thickly corded neck, and looked into his eyes.

"Bram," she said softly, her voice barely audible, "I'll
always cherish this night with you. I'll never regret
it . . ."

He groaned and swept her into his arms, his mouth
descending on her lips, stealing her breath, causing her
heart to thunder as he claimed her. Gradually he broke
their heated kiss, his cobalt eyes burning into her soul,
stealing her heart, infusing her with the joy of total love.
"You were mine from the moment we met," he told her
in a low vibrant voice. "I couldn't take my eyes off you,
Storm. I didn't want to. It was just a matter of time until
now."

Closing her eyes, she swayed back against him. She
felt somehow complete, as she never had before. Her

kiss-swollen lips hinted at a smile. "I want now to last forever."

Bram stroked her cheek, his fingers trembling slightly. "It will, princess," he promised.

They sat near the fire roasting the hot dogs, and then later the marshmallows. Storm leaned against Bram's shoulder, the warmth of the fire lulling her into a peace she had rarely felt since Hal's untimely death. Bram gingerly pulled a charred marshmallow off the stick, blowing on it until it cooled, and then held it close to her lips.

"Last one."

Opening her mouth, she allowed him to feed her. There was something satisfying in the simple gesture. "Mmm, I think I'm going to turn into a fat white marshmallow," she said laughingly, wrapping her arms around her knees.

Bram grinned, his arm resting comfortably around her shoulder, allowing her to lean against him. The flames flickered and danced over the whiteness of the sand, the rest of the world dark and shadowy around them except for the carpet of scintillating stars above. "You could stand to put on a couple of pounds. You're a little too skinny."

Storm nestled contentedly against him. "Hurricane season always leaves you short on sleep and a few pounds lighter."

"I'll be glad when we're out of it," he declared. "Then we can lead a more normal life and see each other a little more often."

She laughed. Their duty consisted of alert every fourth day. Then they had regular administrative duties at the base besides flying, training, or being called in for the special exercises required of every available pilot. "You see me twice or three times a week. Aren't you a glutton for punishment?"

"With Merlin watching us with that know-it-all gleam in his eyes? I can't lean over and kiss you; I can't touch you—" There was flat disgust in his voice. "I don't call that 'seeing' one another."

"Speaking of Merlin, he cornered me the other day and asked me what your intentions were toward me."

Bram looked down at her. "What business is that of his?" he growled.

Storm lifted her chin, looking into his narrowed eyes. "You've got to remember, all the guys at the air station are like big brothers watching out for me. Ever since you put that rose on my desk, the word's gotten around." She chuckled.

His scowl deepened. "They're all jealous," he told her. "Every damn last one of them would love to be right here beside you. They're married, and I'm not."

"Boys," she muttered. "Little boys—every last one of you. I feel like a prize marble being fought over."

He gave her a grudging smile. "Of course, I can't blame them."

"That's big of you, Gallagher."

"Don't go getting a smart mouth, Travis."

She pushed away, a glimmer of mischief in her eyes. "Yeah?" she challenged, getting to her knees. "You wouldn't be threatening me, would you?" she taunted good-naturedly. "All right, jet jockey, let's just see what you're really made of!" And with that, Storm leapt lithely to her feet, shoving him backward into the sand. The surprise written on his face was worth the spontaneous gesture on her part. Laughing, Storm whirled away, running down the beach.

"Why, you—" Bram called, shoving himself upright. And then he grinned. She was living up to her name, all right. Okay, if she was that sure of herself, he'd give her a run for her money. "You won't get away with this!" he shouted as she was swallowed up by the darkness. Sprinting through the sand after her, Bram was surprised at her speed and agility. This was a playful side to her he hadn't seen before, and it was tantalizing. His eyes quickly adjusted to the gloom as he left the area of the firelight. Storm was a good distance ahead of him, silhouetted against the thin wash of moonlight. God, she ran like a tireless cheetah, he thought as he ran swiftly to close the distance between them.

He had to run a good half-mile before even getting close to her. Once she had looked quickly across her shoulder and he had seen a smile lingering at the corners of her mouth, her face dampened by perspiration. Bram called on his reserves for a final burst of speed, but just as he got within ten feet of her Storm whirled around to a stop, her long leg arcing out in a graceful kick that barely brushed his chest. Startled, he jerked to a halt, panting hard.

Storm laughed, gulping air, assuming another languid karate position. "Come on!" she teased. "You want me, come and get me!"

He grinned, watching her closely. So, she knew karate. And what a beautifully balanced body she possessed, he thought, watching her. Her limbs gleamed in the moonlight, each movement fluidly melting into the next. "How long have you been doing that?" he asked.

"A long time."

"What color belt are you, show-off?"

Her teeth gleamed against her honey-colored skin. "Fourth-degree black. Come on, want to try and take me?"

Bram made a lunge for her. Instantly, in a breathtaking feat of athletic control, she leapt upward, both feet in the air, her left leg shooting outward, again lightly brushing his chest. Storm landed perfectly balanced, spinning around to face him. Again he tried, but she was deadly with her feet. He got nowhere. Finally he stopped trying, laughing so hard it hurt. Storm joined him, throwing herself into his arms, kissing him repeatedly. Together they fell to the dark sand, inches from the foaming surf, their laughter mingling with the roar of the ocean around them.

He rolled Storm on top of him, running his hands down her long beautifully formed back. "You're something else," he said, smiling up at her. "I'm impressed as hell. Is that what you did to keep all the men away from your door until I came along?"

She tried to struggle out of his arms, laughing. "You conceited jet jockey!" she gasped. "I might have known you'd think that! Let go of me, Bram Gallagher!"

He dodged her flailing hand. "Not on your life, honey. I don't aim to get kicked by one of your lovely feet. Now come here . . ." He slid his fingers through her hair, gently wrapping it in his hand and rolling her down onto the sand, kissing her long and hard. Her lips were salty, her mouth sweet with the taste of marshmallow. Her breasts rose and fell swiftly, and he could feel the birdlike flutter of her heart against his chest as he deepened the kiss. Storm was warm, alive, yielding, and so much woman that it made him tremble with longing for her once again. She was part playful child, but part proud woman who made no excuse for what she was or was not. He knew in that liquid moment that he loved her completely, unequivocally, and forever.

The next five days were a precious interlude with Bram that was interrupted by Hurricane Brian bearing down on them from the gulf with a vengeance. The six H-52 helicopters were in constant use, and the fifty seasoned Coast Guard pilots were being used up faster than any of them were able to get proper crew rest before flying again.

Storm ran for the safety of the hangar, her flight suit soaked before she made it inside. She walked tiredly down the long crosswalk between the busy crews repairing and preflighting the helicopters for coming missions.

Bram was already in the Ops center when she entered. Kyle Armstrong was coordinating the duty schedule that was filled with more SAR cases than they could handle. Storm thought Kyle's lean face looked drawn. But didn't everyone's? Including hers. Bram roused himself from his thoughtful posture as he studied the chart on the wall. His blue eyes warmed with unspoken affection as Storm met his gaze. She mustered a small smile; it was filled with a silent answering tenderness for him alone.

"Coffee?" Bram asked her, already moving over to the pot.

"Please," she replied thankfully, and walked over to the Ops desk.

"You look better than all of us put together, Stormie," Kyle said, handing her the next case they would fly.

Bram ambled over, handing her a cup, a smile lingering in his eyes. He knew why she looked so good, and Storm had trouble covering up her own smile as she slid her fingers around the mug. Just the slight touch of Bram's long strong fingers made her heart leap. How could she forget that wonderful night on the beach? The love they had shared between them had been pure and honest. It was a complete giving to each other without any games.

"I'd rather fly in a hurricane than have to handle drug smugglers," she told Kyle, studying the report.

The pilot gave her a commiserating look. "You got one there," he agreed.

Bram leaned over her shoulder, reading the report. Storm was acutely aware of his maleness, and she had to make a conscious effort to concentrate on the paper and ignore him. Once he turned his head, his blue eyes probing, disturbing and sensual. Sipping the coffee,

Storm shot him a disgruntled look of warning. Bram knew how much he affected her—damn him!—and he was enjoying that bit of power over her a little too much.

"We're going to relieve the 1406?" Bram asked.

"Yes. They're running low on fuel." Kyle glanced up at both of them. "It's going to be a sector search," he warned them.

Storm groaned. "A sector search?" That meant Bram would also be busy with navigation duties. Imaginary grid lines were drawn over the sea in the supposed area of the lost ship and then followed with the use of instruments and navigation. While it was one of the most accurate patterns for aircraft searching alone, it was twice as hard to fly the lines in inclement weather.

"Sorry, Stormie. This is where we bite the bullet and earn our wings. We've got a fifty-foot yacht called the *Rambler* adrift out in this area." He pointed to the large chart behind him. "We're spread thin and can only allot one helicopter to this assignment."

Storm rubbed her brow, shifting her weight to one booted foot. "What about Clearwater air base over at Tampa? Can't they throw an H-3 our way? It has more search capability than our 52s."

"No go. They're just as busy on that side of the state as we are on ours. Research Coordinating Center Miami is asking some of the northeastern air bases to send all available helicopters and crews down here to try and give us some relief. Man, this damn hurricane has really caught everyone off guard. So many boats were out for weekend fishing even though they were warned about Brian."

"Typical mañana mentality," Storm muttered, running her fingers through her drying hair. It was one of their most frustrating problems: Fishermen tended to disregard the seriousness and destructiveness of a hurricane. And when it hit, the boats were stranded at sea, putting an unnecessary burden on Coast Guard personnel. The "mañana mentality" of "oh, the weather will pass and I'll be safe" endangered themselves and their rescuers. She pulled herself back to the present situation. "Okay, a sector search. What else?"

"The *Rambler's* last report to our station was that there were six people aboard and they were taking in water faster than they could pump it out. The engine aboard the yacht isn't working, so they're at the mercy of the current."

Bram frowned. "I don't think I even want to hear the weather report."

"You won't, Bram. We've got thirty-foot waves out there, and the wind's an erratic bastard at best."

"That means spray coming off the top of those waves," Storm thought out loud. It meant visibility was going to be moderately to severely reduced. She had made rescues where she could not see outside the windows of the 52 because of the blinding spray. Her face became grimmer. "The other crew hasn't spotted the *Rambler?*"

"Negative. Okay, let's get down to the brass tacks here so you can get out there," Kyle said briskly.

Storm lifted the 52 off into the buffeting winds around the air station. Hurricane Brian's outer arms were creating sporadic but violent wind shifts and gusts, making the handling of the helicopter constant continuous work. Merlin took his position at the window by the cabin door in the center of the helicopter, assuming lookout position. Once they were on track, they began searching the angry sea below as they followed the imaginary search pattern lines. The tension in the cabin was palpable as Bram kept calling off the coordinates to her. Five-hundred feet below them the sea was a churning gray-green mistress with waves hungrily grasping skyward with wicked intensity.

"Looks bad down there," Storm said to no one in particular.

"Amen," Merlin chimed in. "Man, if that yacht's still floating, it's gonna be a miracle."

Storm's arms and fingers ached after the first thirty minutes of flying back and forth on the search pattern track. Meticulously accurate navigation in a situation like this was an absolute must. Even the slightest error in longitude or latitude could carry them away from the search area, and six lives could be lost. Bram bent over the instruments, navigation charts resting on his thighs as he concentrated on the most important task of a rescue mission.

"Target at five o'clock, two-hundred yards!" Merlin cried out excitedly.

Storm slowed and turned the bucking, shuddering 52. Squinting into the gray noontime light, she saw the *Rambler.* She heard Bram curse softly.

"Merlin, get that rescue platform ready. We're going to need it," he said.

Her lips tautened into a thin line as she dropped the 52 closer to the strewn wreckage of the once-beautiful yacht. Five bright-orange life vests were visible, with people clinging to the hull of the overturned boat. Storm's gray eyes narrowed as she jockeyed the 52 into a slow circle around the boat as Bram relayed the vital information to the air station.

"Do you see six people, Merlin?" she asked.

"Negative. Only five."

"Damn."

Bram twisted his head, glancing over at her. "What do you want to do?"

"The wind's erratic, but we've got to try lowering a basket. We've got five people in a concentrated area."

The basket was lowered from the crane hoist attached to the helo fuselage. Only two of the five were able to crawl into the wire basket to be hoisted. The other three were so weakened, they could not even grab the basket. Storm chewed on her lower lip, reviewing a number of alternatives for rescuing the other three. "Let's try to land close enough to pick them up."

"You see those waves?" Bram asked grimly.

"Yeah."

"They're at least forty feet high."

She nodded, tension seeping throughout her body, the adrenaline pouring into her bloodstream, making her heart pound. Oh, God—one wrong movement on the cyclic or collective either while floating in the basin of the troughs or upon lifting momentarily above the waves could kill them all. At the least, she'd lose the 52 to the greedy sea. At worst, they would die. Neither was pleasant to ponder.

"You tell me up or down, Bram. I'm going to have my hands full trying to follow Merlin's instructions. I don't want to divide my concentration between flying and watching those waves coming."

"Roger." He folded the charts up, stuffing them into a pouch behind his seat.

Sweat glistened on her face as she brought the 52 downwind within three-hundred feet of the yacht. Tension thrummed through the helicopter as Merlin donned the gunner's belt, a long nylon harness keeping him tethered to the craft so he wouldn't fall out or off the platform. Storm frowned worriedly. Merlin had been jerked out the door more than once trying to reach a drowning survivor with the long wooden pole with a hook at the end of it. Thank God for the gunner's belt, at least.

"Okay, we're going down," she told them stiffly, measuring the last wave as it sloshed a few feet from the bottom of the 52. With a flick of the wrist and a deft touch to the collective, Storm gently set the helicopter on the ocean's wild surface. Spray immediately covered the windows of the cockpit, making it impossible to see. The wind tore at them, trying to throw the tail of the helicopter around, and Storm had to adjust to it by manipulating the foot pedals with her boots.

Merlin slid the door open, releasing the platform so it gave him three more feet for walking out on to try and reach the people who were now screaming frantically for help.

"Up," Bram told her, his voice low.

Storm raised the 52, the wave sloughing by like a predatory animal intent on dragging them downward.

"Down."

And so it went. She had not only to deal with the weather, but to listen to Bram's instructions as well as Merlin's yell above the roar of ocean, rotor blades, and people clinging to the hull only five feet away. Sweat trickled down from her armpits, soaking into her flight suit. Her gloves became damp with sweat, and she held the cyclic and collective more firmly, afraid that if her grip slipped, it would send them all to a watery grave.

"Damn," Bram snarled, watching as Merlin tried to get the first survivor off the hull and onto the platform. The yacht shifted, momentarily trapping the people. Storm brought the helo solidly against the boat, which was now beginning to break up. The survivors crawled across the hull, desperately heading toward them. Merlin leaned out, fingers stretched, yelling at them to crawl closer. "He's going to need help, Storm."

Her gray eyes were troubled. Under such conditions, another helicopter and crew was needed to help in the rescue. But they were all out on individual SAR cases. There was only one gunner's belt. Bram would be back there with no guarantee that he wouldn't fall out into the angry ocean. Her alternatives were limited: Either she left the remaining three people or— No, she couldn't release Bram to go back there and help. As copilot, he was her second set of eyes and ears. Without him up front to help her gauge when to lift off or miss the next wave, it might spell sure death for them. It was suicidal.

What should she do? If she left them and waited for help, the remaining people might drown. If she released Bram, they might all die. But one of the three survivors was a child. . . . Anxiety surged through her. She didn't want to lose Bram either. God, she couldn't take it! Not again. . . .

"Storm?"

"Be careful, Bram."

He gave her a sudden tender look as he unsnapped his harness. "You bet I will, princess. Think you can handle watching the waves? I'll tell you when to lift off from the platform."

"Okay."

He patted her tense shoulder. "I'll hook up to the intercom when I get back there."

For the next fifteen agonizing minutes, Storm fought to keep the valiant 52 steady amid the turbulent sea around them. Four of the five survivors were now aboard, huddled in shock within the blankets. Sweat trickled down her brow, running into her eyes, making them smart. Hurry, hurry! she screamed silently. It was an incredible game of tag with a merciless ocean that sought to deluge them with murderous waves and a relentless wind that slammed repeatedly into the copter. Sea spray was being whipped into the helo, soaking everyone and everything.

"Closer!" Merlin yelled, standing precariously out on the platform. He extended his arm, motioning for the last woman to let go and crawl the necessary two feet to the helicopter platform. Finally a wave broke her hold on the hull, and she bobbed like a cork swallowed into the sucking grasp of the ocean. Bram grimly watched the woman flail. She was hysterical, her movements jerky and uncoordinated. Instead of striking out with steady strokes toward them, she foundered, at the mercy of the current.

"Close in on her, Lieutenant Travis!" Merlin said. "She's panicking."

Gingerly, with a feather-light touch, Storm allowed the 52 to move sideways, closing the distance between them. "Up!" Bram yelled, warning Merlin to hold on. The 52 moved upward, fighting the screaming wind, trying to crest above the next wave. Seawater slammed into the sponsons below the belly of the copter, making them shudder drunkenly. Dammit! Storm chastised herself. The waves were not a constant uniform height. They ranged anywhere from forty to fifty feet. It was hard to judge their height and simultaneously keep everything else under control.

"Down," Bram shouted. Quickly Storm maneuvered the 52 back toward the woman in the water.

Merlin cursed. "Man, she's outta her head, Lieutenant Gallagher." He tried to motion for her to swim toward them, but it was hopeless. Only five feet separated them.

Bram unsnapped his helmet, setting it on the deck. Quickly he jerked the two cords that inflated the life vest he was wearing. Grabbing the trail line, he tied it around him. Getting out of his boots, he gripped Merlin's arm. "I'll go in after her. Watch the waves for Lieutenant Travis. Just keep a firm grip on this line . . ."

"She's in a panic, sir," Merlin warned, screaming above the wind and rotors.

"No!" Storm yelled. "Bram—don't do it!"

With his helmet off, he was no longer in communication with her. Merlin started to relay the message, but the officer had already dived into the murky water before he could say anything.

Storm's heart lurched with anger and fear. Bram shouldn't have done it! But another part of her said Yes, he had to. She knew better. More than one crewman had dived into water to save survivors. But this time . . . this time it was the man she loved. That thought slammed into her, leaving Storm close to tears.

"Up!" Merlin cried.

She wrenched back on the controls. More spray and seawater slapped at the underbelly of the 52. Damn, the waves were getting larger!

Storm's throat ached with unremitting tension as she watched Bram fight his way through the violent water toward the last survivor. Her attention was torn between three separate functions, and she could not risk concentrating on Bram any longer. Merlin would have to orchestrate the rescue of Bram and the woman. An icy fear gripped her as she begged, coaxed, and swore at the 52 under her breath, coordinating the macabre dance on the ocean's surface. Another three minutes passed before Merlin was able to use the long wooden pole to snag Bram's outstretched hand and pull him aboard with the unconscious woman in his arms.

"Get her up!" Merlin cried, slamming the door shut against the howling fury of the hurricane.

Grimly Storm wrenched the 52 skyward with its heavy load. The helicopter strained mightily, the whine of the turbine increasing in screeching protest as she banked, heading upward, away from the hellish sea below them. Radioing in, Storm was too busy for the first five minutes to divide her attention between her duties and the cabin.

"Storm—" It was Bram's gasping voice. "Call base. ...Tell them to stand by with an ambulance. . . ."

Swiftly Storm risked a glance back, aware of the anguish in his voice. Merlin and Bram were both kneeling over the last survivor, giving her mouth-to-mouth resuscitation. Storm compressed her lips and returned to the job at hand, forcing the tears back. Her hands tightened around the controls. She silently willed the woman to live. She had probably swallowed too much seawater, her lungs full of the brackish liquid. Thank God, Bram was safe. Forcing all those thoughts aside, Storm cranked up the engine on the 52, keeping an eye on the engine temperature gauge. The needle hovered unsteadily between the safety of the green region and the danger area of the red. The turbine engine of the 52 was actually too powerful for the helicopter transmission, and if a pilot unwisely pushed the engine past its limits, the torque could cause flight control problems.

Storm was so intent on monitoring the performance of the 52, she didn't realize Bram had come forward until his hand settled briefly on her shoulder. A quick glance over at his pale glistening features made her heart wrench with fear.

"How is she?"

"Looks like about a quart of water came from her lungs. She's breathing on her own, but she doesn't look good," he informed her, strapping in.

"And you?"

He glanced over at her, a tight grin pulling one corner of his mouth upward as he wiped his face. "I drank a quart of water just trying to rescue her."

Storm found no humor in the situation. "You could have drowned out there, Bram."

As he pulled the charts from the pocket to help in navigation, he gave her a narrowed look. "That's part of our job."

Chilling anger caused her gray eyes to glimmer like chips of ice. She refused to answer him, burying all her emotions. The twenty-minute flight back to the air station was completed in tense silence.

Storm finished the postflight check and was the last to leave the confines of the helicopter once they had landed. In the meantime, Bram and Merlin had helped the survivors into the two waiting ambulances. Tucking her helmet into her duffel bag, Storm jogged to the line shack.

Bram was soaked and so was Merlin. They all looked like drowned rats. None of them looked particularly dynamic under the circumstances. Walking back into the Ops Center, Kyle's face was grimmer than before.

"All hell's breaking loose here," he told them. "We're getting your aircraft refueled in the hangar right now. We need all available equipment. Merlin, you'd better get in another supply of rescue items."

"Yes, sir." Merlin shook his head dolefully, making an about face and leaving Ops.

Storm felt as if she were about to snap. "What now, Kyle?"

"We've got a freighter in trouble. I've got 1378 on the way. We've got twenty crew members to get off that ship before it sinks."

Swearing softly, Storm rapidly read through the report. It was now 1500 and the day was looking even more bleak and overcast. Though it was midafternoon, it appeared to be dusk. Visibility was quickly deteriorating, and that meant IFR flying in a few hours—just one more overtaxing demand on her and Bram. Her mind was tired, and she felt numb. Stealing a glance over at Bram, she felt a moment's reprieve from the inner turmoil she was experiencing.

"Look, grab some coffee, and I'll have the rest of the info radioed to you while you're on your way to the freighter."

"What's its registry?"

"Panamanian."

Storm sighed heavily. "Could be Colombian drug smugglers who came up the coast to drop their goods off on smaller boats and got caught in this damned hurricane. That's the usual pattern, isn't it?"

Kyle soberly agreed. "RCC says they can barely speak English. I hope Merlin has brushed up on his Spanish."

"Bram can handle it," she told him, scooping up the search briefing papers.

Kyle looked at his watch. "Look, you two have completed four-and-a-half hours of demanding flying. You've done your bit, and you both look pretty beat."

"Thanks a lot," Storm said, feeling more and more tense by the second. She looked up at Bram, who gave her a cup of the lifesaving coffee. "What do you want to do?" He looked like hell, his face drawn and pale. Rescuing the woman in that heavy ocean current had taken a drastic toll on him physically. His blue eyes glimmered with a sudden tender light that made her feel warm and safe within his regard.

"You're the AC. I'm game if you are."

She thought for a moment. He should be left behind, considering his present condition. But the look in his eyes told her he could handle it.

"We'll do it, Kyle."

A look of relief washed across Armstrong's features. "Thank God. Frankly, I don't know what I would have done if you said no."

Reaching out, Storm squeezed Kyle's arm. "Thanks for giving us a choice though . . ."

7

They sat in the helicopter, preparing to lift off again. Bram looked over at her.

"Let me fly for a while. You need a break."

"Fine," Storm agreed, pulling the navigation charts out and placing them on her lap.

"What's wrong, Storm?"

Her answer was clipped, emotionless. "Nothing."

Bram stared at her, appraising her unreadable features. He saw the strain in the set of her lips, the look of tension in her eyes. "You're pissed off about something."

Storm snapped her chin up, glaring at him. "I said it was nothing, dammit. Now, let it go at that. We've got work to do."

He studied her grimly, as if not convinced by her anger. "Okay," he responded, "but later you and I are going to talk."

She said nothing, avoiding his piercing look. Damn him. Didn't he realize how worried she was for him when he left the helicopter? He knew she was sensitive to losing another copilot. But this time there was so much more at stake: She loved him. And he didn't know that. Finally she chanced a glance over at Bram. He coolly met her stare.

"Sometimes you're an insensitive rock," she said grimly.

"Yeah?"

"Yes!"

"You're barking up the wrong tree, Storm."

"Bull."

"You hotheaded—"

"Let's cut out the pleasantries, Bram, and get this show on the road. We can call each other names after this damned flight is over with."

"Okay, if that's the way you want to play it. You damn well better be prepared to explain yourself when we get back."

The freighter *Antonia* foundered like a beached whale in the Atlantic Ocean below them. CG 1378 was already on station, using the rescue basket, which was being lowered to the crewman anxiously standing below on the heaving deck of the ship. Storm recognized the voice of Doug Sanders, the pilot of 1378. They circled, watching the problems that were occurring. The wind was whipping in a tight concentric pattern, throwing the rescue basket around like a toy beneath the H-52. If it slammed into one of the waiting Colombian crewmen huddling on the bow of the sinking freighter, it could kill one of them.

"CG 1446," came the call to Storm over the radio.

"Go ahead, CG 1378."

"CG '46 . . . hey, Stormie! Glad to have you out here with us. I thought you were on another SAR."

She smiled thinly. "We just completed it and got sent

right back out. Looks like you're having trouble, Doug."

"Roger that. These damn Colombians we've already got on board are crazier than hell. They're hysterical. Already had two or three of them below try to hang on to the basket all at once. My mech's been trying to use hand signals to tell them we'll lift them one at a time. They aren't paying much attention."

"How many do you have on board, Doug?"

"Three. They look like smugglers. I'll bet you my next paycheck on it."

She shook her head, maneuvering the helo in a wide circle above the other 52. She felt Bram's hand on her arm and she turned.

"I speak Spanish fluently. How about if I go down on deck and organize them for the rescue?"

Her eyes widened for a brief second. Come on, Storm, separate work from emotional fears, she told herself. "Think you can manage it? You look tired. . . ."

Bram gave her his devastating grin that always brought a smile to her face. She didn't smile this time, but he saw her gray eyes lighten momentarily. "Sure, as long as a war doesn't break out down there. They don't look like a very trustworthy lot."

"War never determines who's right, Bram—only who is left. Make damn sure you're left."

His grin broadened. "You're a pretty savvy lady, you know that? Yes, I'll be careful. I'll take one of those portable watertight radios with me and stay in contact." He winked and unstrapped, giving her shoulder a gentle squeeze, and left the cockpit for the gloomy interior of the helicopter.

Storm watched him go with misgivings. More than once she had wished mightily for the reassurance of a weapon on board—especially around the drug smugglers, who they had to rescue or round up in coordi-

nated busts with the cutter crews who prowled the sea
for them. She radioed Doug, outlining their plan. Relief
was evident in the pilot's voice as he agreed to it. Both
H-52s were low on fuel and couldn't stay on station
much longer. Something had to be done quickly to
effect the rescue.

In a matter of minutes, Doug had pulled away from
the *Antonia,* allowing Storm to lower her copilot in the
basket to the deck of the ship. Waves crashed across the
bow, and she worriedly watched as the crewmen clung
desperately to the railing, trying not to be washed
overboard. Bram's bright-orange flight suit and white
helmet stood out among the Colombians, who quickly
surrounded him as he got out of the basket. He was tall
and huskily built next to the smaller crewmen, and
Storm smiled to herself as Bram quickly organized
them. It wasn't long before Merlin was hoisting them
aboard, one at a time. In fifteen minutes, eight bodies
were packed closely together inside the confines of the
aircraft. Storm maneuvered the weighted helicopter
away from the badly battered *Antonia* so that Doug
could move in and pick up the rest. She heard Merlin
snapping and yelling at the crew, and she twisted
around to find out what was going on.

The largest sailor was gesturing angrily toward Merlin, shouting in Spanish at him. Dammit, she wished
Bram were aboard—his bulk could intimidate them into
silence.

"Hey, Stormie, I've got my quota," Doug sang
through the airwaves. "All you need to do is go back
and pick up Bram and we'll have it made. I'm a little
overweight, or I'd do it."

"Roger," she said, watching as the 1378 backed out
of the area so she could pick up Bram. He looked alone
and lost down on the deck awash with debris from the
freighter.

"Merlin, stand by to lower the basket—" Her voice

froze as the caution panel lit up for a TRANSMISSION OIL HOT indication. Her eyes widened, moving to the gauge. The needle was resting in the red, meaning the transmission was overheating! Anxiously she went through the customary checks to see if it was a real emergency or just the gauge acting up. Merlin came forward, crouching down near her. His face became drawn as he looked at the flight instruments.

"We've got trouble," he warned her, pointing to them.

"Yeah, I know."

"We're slightly overloaded, lieutenant. Beyond our eight-thousand-pound capacity."

Storm twisted around, glaring at the crewmen in the back. "Dammit, we shouldn't be! What the hell are they carrying? Search them, Merlin. We should be able to take one more person on board without this happening."

Her mind feverishly raced over the reasons for the problem. With high humidity and temperature conditions, coupled with high-powered hovering, the helo's engine was laboring. Being overloaded weight-wise was the straw that placed them in a critical situation.

She radioed Doug, asking him to stand by.

"I can't," he told her, "I'm into my half-hour's reserve of extra fuel, Storm. I've got to go. You've got to come with me. If your transmission overheats and you get any other indications that it's coming apart, you're going to have to ditch."

"Bram's down there," she said, desperation in her voice. She heard a disturbance behind her and turned her head. Merlin shoved the only huge Colombian crewman down on the deck of the helicopter, yanking up his voluminous shirt, exposing a belt filled with white plastic pouches strapped around his waist.

"Goddamn thieves," he snarled, "they're all carrying cocaine on them, lieutenant!"

117

Cursing, Storm radioed the air station, apprising them of the situation. Did any of those idiotic crewmen have a weapon? A cold horror raised the hair on the back of her neck at that thought. It was usual for a smuggler to carry firearms. Anxiously Storm flew over the *Antonia,* watching Bram cling to the safety of one of the masts. Wave after wave inundated the ship, and tears rose in her eyes. The caution light stayed on, compounding the peril.

"I got it all, lieutenant. Man, there must be over fifty pounds of coke on them."

"Dump it!" she ordered.

Merlin slid the door open, the wind and rain whipping into the helicopter. The crewmen yelled and started to lunge forward as he began to kick the drugs overboard in order to lighten the load. Merlin punched the closest one in the jaw, sending the crewman sprawling back among his protesting friends.

"It's out!" Merlin gasped, slamming the door shut once again. He glared at the crewmen and dared them to try anything.

The transmission temperature gauge was still high. Storm's mouth thinned, her eyes narrowing. "No good; we're still riding the red."

"Storm," Doug begged over the radio, "let's go. I'm down to twenty-five minutes of fuel left! We'll refuel and come back to get Bram. He'll be okay down there."

Tears crowded her eyes, but she fought them back. Daylight was dying. Armstrong had informed her that no other helicopters were available to help rescue Bram—every one of them was out on a critical lifesaving mission. She thumbed the button on the cyclic, putting her in touch with Bram down below.

"I can't pick you up, Bram. I've got transmission problems. We're going to have to come back just as soon as we change planes and refuel."

"Roger," he answered.

Storm shut her eyes tightly for a second. God, he sounded so calm and nonchalant about it! That ship could break apart at any given moment. He could be washed overboard by a monster wave. He could drown. He—

"The war's finished and I'm left, Storm. I'll be hanging around here waiting for you."

Swallowing hard, her voice came back, hoarse and raw. "Roger. ETA will be," she glanced at her watch, "one hour and ten minutes."

She heard him laugh. It was a full carefree laugh that sent a spasm of anguish through her. "You got a date, princess. See you in seventy minutes."

"I'll be there," she promised grimly and ordered Merlin to throw out a Datum Marker Buoy. She pulled the 52 up and banked it to the left.

"If you don't, I'll turn into a pumpkin," Bram warned.

It was his last communication. Between the screaming and fighting going on between Merlin and the furious Colombian crew, and limping home on a transmission that she wasn't sure would complete the flight, Storm doggedly flew the helicopter back to the air base. On landing, they were met by Customs authorities who willingly took the crewmen into custody. Storm ran to the hangar. She jerked the door to Ops open. Kyle glanced up.

"We're refueling Doug's helicopter right now," he said by way of greeting.

Storm looked down at him, her face devoid of emotion, her gray eyes dark. "I'm going back after him, Kyle."

"You're in the bag, Storm. I'll send—"

She slammed her hand down flatly on the desk and glared at Kyle face-to-face. "I'm going back for him. Let me be Doug's copilot on this flight. We'll use his mech, Anderson. Merlin fought those Colombians all the way back; he's exhausted."

"Okay, you'll be copilot on this flight," he agreed.

Storm's taut face relaxed slightly. "Thanks, Kyle. I owe you one." Anytime a pilot flew six hours of flight time, they were automatically "in the bag" and taken off the duty roster to rest for at least twelve hours before attempting to fly again. Her gray eyes softened as she stared across the desk at Kyle.

"Just be damned careful, Storm. You look like hell. You're tired, and mistakes are real easy to come by when you're in this kind of a bind. My ass is on the line on this one."

"I will."

Doug took one look at Storm and said, "I'll fly, you navigate."

"You've got a deal," she agreed tiredly, quickly strapping in. "How many hours have you been flying?"

He grinned, his lean face breaking the lines of tension around his mouth. "Not as many as you, that's for sure. Did all hell break loose in your helo too?"

"Yeah, Merlin found coke on them."

Doug gave a sorrowful shake of his head. "Dumb bastards. You might have had to ditch because of the excess weight. You should have thrown one of them out. Okay, let's get Bram."

The forty minutes it took to follow the track to the drifting *Antonia* was an agonizing eternity for Storm. The long day was ending, darkness beginning to steal over the sky. The rain and wind slashed relentlessly at the helicopter as Doug tracked outbound one-thousand feet above the ocean surface. Luckily Bram was still in radio communication with a circling U.S. Navy P3B that flew high above him. Storm forced herself to relax and stop worrying; she had to unclench her fists every few minutes. She was sorry for snapping at Bram earlier. It was concern for his life that had made her testy. Please, please, she prayed silently, keep him safe. I love him.

"Target at three o'clock, one-hundred yards," the flight mech sang out.

Storm strained against her harness, craning to get a good look at the darkened shape of the *Antonia* rapidly coming into view. Her heart rate rose to a throbbing pound as they neared the listing vessel.

"Thirteen-seventy-eight, it's about time," Bram called over the radio. "I'm getting soaked down here!"

Relief washed through her, and she shared a smile with Doug.

"You mean you didn't turn into a pumpkin yet?" Storm responded.

Bram's laughter was hearty, uplifting. "No, but I've turned into a toad instead. I need to be kissed by my princess in order to turn back into a handsome prince."

"That guy is something else," Doug said, shaking his head. "You want to fly, Storm?"

"No, not as long as you're feeling okay. I'm getting groggy, Doug."

"Roger. You look like death warmed over."

"Thanks a lot. You really know how to boost a woman's flattened ego."

Doug grinned and directed the 52 until they hovered twenty feet above the *Antonia*. Below, Bram waited for the basket to be lowered, clinging to the same broken mast where they had left him. Doug gave Storm a broad smile. "I think your copilot will have some pretty sweet words for you when he gets aboard."

Storm felt her cheeks warm with color. "Now, what's that supposed to mean?"

"Come on, Stormie, we aren't blind, deaf, and

dumb," he chided good-naturedly. "We may be married men, but we can tell when a guy's falling in love with our favorite lady pilot."

She colored fiercely, avoiding Doug's humored blue-eyed gaze. Bram falling in love with her? He was still gun-shy from his recent divorce and afraid of entrusting his vulnerable emotions to any woman's care again. He had told her that in so many words on the beach. Frowning, she was too exhausted to parry Doug's comment. Yes, they had shared wonderful love together. And carefree laughter . . . and . . . did he love her? Rubbing her eyes, she shook her head.

There was a sudden blast of wind and rain as Bram struggled aboard, collapsing on the deck. Doug motioned for Storm to unharness and go back to assist. She gave him a grateful nod and unstrapped. Anderson was helping Bram to his feet when she came back. Storm placed her hands beneath his left arm and led him to the canvas and nylon webbed seats along the fuselage wall. His hands trembled as he weakly pulled the helmet off his head, letting it fall from his nerveless fingers onto the deck. He felt Storm close to him, providing him with badly needed support. He allowed his head to tip back against the wall and closed his eyes, water running in rivulets down his exhausted features.

Anderson handed her two towels and got up, placing a heavy wool blanket around Bram's broad sloping shoulders.

"Thanks," he whispered tiredly, giving him a weary smile. Then he turned his head to the left, meeting Storm's serious expression. "God, am I glad you're here. You're a sight for sore eyes, sweetheart."

She took the towel, trying to dry his hair, and wipe his face and neck free of the water. Her heart soared with joy as his blue eyes hungrily drank in her form.

"Trite, Gallagher, but effective," she said, a slight smile pulling at her lips.

"Can't be original all the time, princess."

She wrapped the towel around his neck, tucking it into the open V of his flight suit.

"You're an original, all right, you damn ex–fighter jock."

He barely opened his eyes, one brow moving upward. "Hey, haven't I earned being called a Red Tail yet? If the guys back in my fighter squadron could have seen me getting seasick and clinging for dear life from the mast of that freighter, they'd have never believed it. I think I earned my water wings today, Travis."

Storm wanted to reach out and caress his face, but the circumstances didn't permit it. Instead she contented herself with simply remaining close to him. "You're right," she said above the noise, "you are officially a Coastie as of today, lieutenant. Now quit bitching and rest—you're shaking like a leaf."

"You're coming home with me," Storm said, brooking no argument from Bram. With the continuing crisis of the hurricane, all pilots were being given the mandatory twenty-four-hours crew rest before returning to fly SAR missions again.

Bram raised one eyebrow as they left the hangar, then bowed his head against the tempestuous rain. He was wet, cold, tired, and hungry. "No argument," he shouted above the wind, following Storm to her sports car. Once inside, he fell back against the seat and closed his eyes.

"What you need is a bath, hot food, and rest," she advised, easing the car out into the rain-soaked street.

"Amen," he agreed. He fumbled for her hand, and on finding it, gave it a squeeze. "You are wonderful, Storm Travis," he sighed.

She worriedly looked over at Bram's pale features. Maybe Kyle had been right—they should have ordered Bram to the dispensary for examination. But he had resisted Kyle's suggestion, and they were all too tired to argue. "Rest, Bram," she murmured.

Just getting away from the air base with its continual strain of flying infused her with a new kind of strength. Bram was far more exhausted than he had originally let on. Getting battered by forty-foot waves for over an hour and a half had depleted even his herculean strength. Storm led him to the bathroom, started running the bathwater, and stripped him of the smelly, damp flight suit. He remained in a weary stupor, even the simple task of unlacing his flight boots proving to be too much. Kneeling down, Storm quickly removed the boots and soaked socks and placed them aside.

"Come on," she urged, gripping his arm and helping him stand, "the water's ready."

She left Bram soaking in the tub. Changing out of her flight suit, she slipped into a robe and moved through the familiar task of preparing a quick meal. It was like being married again. Storm shook her head as a tender smile began pulling at her lips. She heated the rich beef stew she had made a few days earlier. Was she enjoying these domestic tasks because it was familiar or because Bram was with her once again? A little of both, she admitted ruefully to herself.

Reentering the bathroom, she found Bram asleep in the tub. An understanding smile touched her mouth. Getting down on her knees, she rolled up the sleeves on her robe and began to scrub him free of the salty ocean smell. He awoke, groggily opening his eyes and sitting up.

"Here," he mumbled, "I can do that—"

"Just sit there," she told him. "I can do it faster and quicker than you can."

He rubbed his face and then wet his dark hair. "I feel like hell. Where's the shampoo?"

"Here," she said, putting it firmly into his hand.

"Thanks." He began to wash his hair.

"I've got beef stew ready and some garlic bread out in the kitchen. Do you feel like eating?"

"I'm so damned hungry I'm shaky."

She smiled, rinsing off his beautifully muscled chest and shoulders. It was a provocative task, and if they hadn't been exhausted, it might have led to other pleasures. Storm gently put those wishes aside, helping him stand and extricate himself from the tub without falling on his face. He was like a sleepy little boy, fumbling for the towel, his movements slow and unco-ordinated. After getting him dry, she took another towel and wrapped it around his waist. Taking his hand, Storm led him into the kitchen.

"You go ahead and eat," she urged, placing the steaming bowl of stew before him.

Bram looked up. She looked beautiful in that pale green robe, and it accented her dark gray eyes. Her hair was smooth and straight from wearing the flight helmet for so long, her bangs hanging near her thick lashes. "What about you? Aren't you—"

Storm leaned over, pressing a kiss to his sandpapery cheek. "I'm desperately in need of a shower first. Eat and then go to bed. I'll join you in a little while," she promised softly.

The wind slammed savagely against the house, with the shutters flapping and banging, awakening Bram from his deep sleep. He felt Storm's warm yielding body next to him move, and he inhaled her apricot scent, forcing his eyes open.

The clamor abruptly abated, and peace settled briefly over the darkened room. He was safe. Memories of almost being swept overboard from the *Antonia* at least five different times had haunted his dreams, but he had slept soundly. Bram blinked, opening his eyes. He felt pleasantly tired, not bone-deep tired as before. Twisting his head, he glanced at the clock. Five o'clock in the morning. He looked over at Storm, gently smoothing her hair on the pillow next to where they lay. Propping himself up on one elbow, Bram grimaced, every muscle in his body painfully screaming in protest.

Storm stirred like a lost kitten, automatically reaching out, her hand sliding down across his chest. He smiled; she missed his nearness. With his fingers, he stroked her pale cheek, noticing the strain still evident on her face. He had heard stories about how Coast Guard people were placed under grueling pressure during life-and-death emergencies, but he had never fathomed something of this continuing magnitude. When he had been in the Air Force, everyone had laughed at the "Coasties," viewing them as more of a civilian agency than a military one, because they ended up protecting the civilian populace more than the other armed services did. He had laughed with them, believing they had a cushy job and didn't deserve the respect he now accorded them. Now he knew better.

He pulled his thoughts back to Storm. He loved the velvet texture of her skin beneath his hand as he explored her neck and shoulder. The wind slammed frenziedly against the house, and the rain pounded at the windows, which were shuttered to protect them from the hurricane's flying debris.

Storm moaned, slowly rolling onto her back. Bram's touch had pulled her from sleep and as she raised her lashes she met his tender gaze. "What time is it?" she asked in a sleepy voice.

"0500."

She relaxed, shutting her eyes again, loving his gently stroking touch on her arm and shoulder. "God, I feel like I've been hit by a Mack truck," she muttered thickly. "Are you all right?"

Bram rested his hand against her slender waist. "Not only hit, but run over."

Concern showed in her eyes as she opened them, reaching out and sliding her fingers across his broad shoulder. "Bad?"

He shook his head. "Bruised a little, that's all. How about you?"

Storm struggled into a sitting position, the covers falling away, exposing the white satin nightgown she wore. Her hair had been damp when she had gone to bed, and now it lay about her face in softened waves. "I feel like hell, and I probably look like hell," she admitted. "You look pretty good, Bram."

His cobalt eyes gleamed as he shifted to study her in the muted light. "You look absolutely ravishing," he murmured suggestively. "And if we weren't both so damned exhausted, I'd do something about it."

Storm's eyes widened, and as she wordlessly slid down beside him she placed her arms around his neck and rested her head against his. "Hold me?"

His arms came around her body, pulling her daringly close to his hard length. Storm was aware of his arousal and snuggled further into his strong embrace. "Better?" he asked, kissing her temple, cheek, and finally, her lips.

A new urgency filled her and she hungrily met his questing mouth, wanting, needing, the strength and care he offered.

"Mmm, you taste good," he whispered against her lips. He pressed his mouth against hers more insistently, and felt her lips part beneath his. Fire uncoiled hotly throughout him. Raising his head, he stared down into her pewter eyes, now flecked with the silver flame of desire. "I had a lot of time out on the ship to think," he whispered, pressing small affectionate kisses to her lips.

"I was so afraid for you, Bram," she admitted

throatily, her eyes clouding as she searched his strong, handsome face.

A mocking smile settled over his mouth. "I was scared, if you want to know the truth. When I saw you leaving, I thought What the hell· have you done, Gallagher? Don't you realize this ship can fall apart on you any second?" He shook his head, and his hands tightened on her body. "I suppose any other copilot with an ounce of brains wouldn't have risked it. But I'm a dumb ex–fighter jock, and what the hell do I know about ships and the sea?" he teased.

Storm smiled lovingly and reached up, running her fingers through his hair. "Sometimes what you don't know will save you." She laughed softly. "And what you did, Bram, was to go that extra mile. A lot of the· people in the Coast Guard are like that, though. You fit the Red Tail mold· well."

He inhaled her special female fragrance, nuzzling her ear, lost in the silken texture of her hair against his cheek. "Too bad I risked my tail for a bunch of drug smugglers." He chuckled. "Somehow, doing it for them took some of the satisfaction out of the gesture."

She leaned upward, kissing him soundly, reveling in his natural strength. "It doesn't matter," she told him, closing her eyes, content to be held by him, "you're made of the right stuff. The Coast Guard couldn't have gotten a better pilot if they'd tried."

Bram grinned. "Is that your professional opinion, Lieutenant Travis?"

"Mine and everyone else's," she confided, growing serious. "You're solid gold, Lieutenant Gallagher, but we've been afraid to tell you that because we figured it would go to that already swelled head of yours."

He gave her a nonplussed look and then broke into a solid laugh as he pinned her to the bed beneath him. She was incredibly alluring right now, the silk of her nightgown providing an inviting sensation against his flesh. With one hand he easily captured her wrists above her head.

"You're awfully impertinent, Storm Travis," he said, running his finger down her clean jawline. Then he sobered, staring down at her vulnerable face. "But I'm finding out that's just one more quality that I like about you," he admitted. "Out there on that freighter I had an hour and a half to wonder if I was going to live or die, Storm . . ." His voice dropped to a roughened whisper as he stared down at her. "I had plenty of time to think and to weigh what is and isn't important in my life." He outlined her provocative lips with one finger. "You're important to me. And I wanted to tell you that. When I got aboard the 52 all I wanted to do was throw my arms around you and hold you. I couldn't, but I thought you'd see how I felt about you . . ."

Her heart beat painfully in her chest, and Storm became aware of the tears filling her eyes. "I saw something in your eyes, Bram—I couldn't be sure." She gave him a helpless look. "What I might wish it to be and what it actually was could easily have been different," she added almost inaudibly.

Bram cocked his head, a smile lingering on his lips. "You mean you care a little for me too?"

Tears fled down her cheeks and soaked into the strands of her hair. Storm wanted to blurt out I love you, Bram. I love you so damn much, my heart aches! But she couldn't say it. At least, not yet. Perhaps never. Swallowing the lump forming in her throat, Storm looked above his head into the darkness. "I know you've just come out of a divorce, Bram," she began hoarsely, "and you've made it clear that you don't want any serious relationships right now—"

He released her wrists and cupping her chin, searched her tear-stained face. "I've changed my mind," he murmured, leaning down and kissing her lips. He felt her arms slipping around his shoulders, drawing him down on her warm, yielding body, and he groaned softly against her mouth. "I want to love you."

"Yes . . ." Storm quavered, losing herself within his sensual, masculine aura. "Please, Bram, I need you so much . . . I almost lost you . . ."

"Shh," he remonstrated, running his tongue across her pliant, petal-soft lips, "you'll never lose me, princess. Never."

8

I don't know if I'm ever going to get used to seeing palm trees swaying in seventy-five-degree temperatures at Christmastime," Bram admitted, entering the kitchen, drink in hand. He halted in the doorway and leaned against it, idly watching as Storm put the finishing touches on another tray of appetizers for the party that was in full swing.

Storm glanced up. "Newcomers usually find it strange. You'll get used to it." She smiled, picking up the tray and walking over to where Bram was leaning. "Want to take this in? You'd think those guys had never been fed before."

Bram balanced the tray in his hands along with his drink. "Come on in," he urged. "You throw a party, but your guests never get to see the lady who brought it all about. Come on . . ."

She frowned. "Well—"

"Look, those chow hounds have plenty to eat and

drink in there," he ordered. Then his voice grew tender. "Besides, I'd like to spend some time with you."

Giving him a smile, Storm smoothed the folds of her ivory muslin dress. It had a pink ribbon through the lace of the high collar that fitted around her slender neck. She felt extremely feminine tonight, basking in the light of Bram's sensual gaze. Blushing from the look he gave her, Storm acquiesced. "Okay, I'll join you for a little while. But there're so many other things—"

"Let Betty and Susie help next time." He suddenly grinned, leaning down and catching her full on the mouth, kissing her soundly.

"Aha!" Kyle cried, intercepting them. "Finally caught you two!" A self-satisfied look came to his face as he sauntered up to them.

Storm flushed fiercely, unable to meet Kyle's friendly expression for a moment.

Bram wasn't so easily ruffled by the pilot's exclamation. "Here, Armstrong, you carry this instead of bending your elbow or flapping your jaw."

Kyle laughed and took the tray. "We miss you, Stormie."

"See?" Bram said archly.

"I'm coming!"

The Christmas music mingled with the nonstop laughter and chatter of the twenty couples who had made themselves at home in the living and dining room areas of the house. Bram remained with Storm as she made the rounds as hostess, watching, looking, and listening. A warmth stole over him as his focus rested on Storm—as it always did. He would never tire of looking at her vulnerable, honest features and those wide-set gray eyes that made his body tighten with desire for her again. Had it been five months since meeting and snarling at each other in the hangar on that humid Sunday afternoon?

He smiled, made the appropriate small talk, and

continued to walk at Storm's side. Since that night after his rescue from the *Antonia,* their relationship had subtly changed and deepened. Both were frightened. Both had something to lose by loving again. But their days and nights had been full of emotion. He rubbed his jaw, troubled. He had come to love Storm as he had no other woman. The feelings she brought alive in him were new, strong, and binding. Maggie had never evoked those kinds of feelings from him. But Storm was infinitely different from his ex-wife. Storm was steady, loyal, and sincere. A slight smile suffused his features as he watched the light dance off her ginger hair, copper and gold highlights burnishing the silky strands.

The amount of flying hours they had logged as a team between September and December had been staggering. And through it all, Storm had amazed him with the dogged steadiness that made her a beacon of sureness to all those around her. There wasn't a man here who didn't enjoy flying with her. Bram's eyes softened as he watched her laugh as she shared a joke with one of the wives. He loved Storm's ability to relate to everyone: adult or child, friend or lover. Right now, this very instant, he wanted to grip her hand and take her to the beach and make passionate love to her beneath the light of the moon. It was Christmas—a time of giving, of sharing. As he surveyed the room Bram realized how much all of these people had come to mean to him. There was a sense of family unity in the Coast Guard that just wasn't found in the other services. It was like finally coming home.

It was nearly two A.M. before the last couple reluctantly left. Storm flopped down on the nearest couch, giving Bram a pleased look as he came and joined her.

"You know how to throw a successful party," Bram congratulated, meeting her tired smile. "No one wanted to leave."

She reached out, sliding her fingers down his hard, muscular arm, relishing his closeness. "I loved it. Thanks for helping me make it a success."

Bram nodded. "We work well as a team," he agreed, looking at the brightly lit Christmas tree that stood well over six feet tall in the corner of the living room.

"I'm exhausted," she admitted, leaning back on the couch and closing her eyes. Then she opened them and surveyed the room. "And this place has to be cleaned up. . . ."

"Not tonight," he warned her.

She turned her head toward him, basking in the light of his tender gaze. "Stay over tonight?"

"I was planning on it."

"Good."

He got to his feet and pulled her into his arms.

Storm leaned against him, marveling at his seemingly inexhaustible strength. Nuzzling beneath his chin, she was content to remain there, luxuriating in his touch as he gently massaged her neck and shoulders with his large gentle hands. Their time had been rare precious moments stolen from the fabric of their demanding work. And lately she had craved more time alone with Bram to explore him, his life, and what he wanted from the future. The midnight walks on the beach were their special time with each other and more than once they had made love on the white sands that cradled them lovingly.

"Just think," she said wistfully, "we have Christmas Eve and Christmas off. I can't believe it. In all my years in the service I've never lucked out on major holidays."

Bram chuckled. "Yeah, I was the same way. I knew without a doubt if there was a holiday coming up, I'd get nailed with the duty. Never failed." He pulled away, keeping his hands on her shoulders, staring down at her. "Merry Christmas," he said huskily, leaning down and touching her lips in a long exploratory kiss.

Storm drank thirstily of his mouth, reveling in the firmness yet sensitivity conveyed through his touch. Gazing up into his eyes, she implored, "Take me to the beach. I want time alone with you, Bram."

A mirthful glint shone in his eyes. "At two in the morning? It's going to be chilly down there. Do you want to change first?"

She nodded. "Yes, give me a minute." And then she reached up, kissing him soundly. "Thank you," she whispered fiercely.

They walked arm in arm on the darkened sand, watching the ocean spill its foamy life out onto the sloping shore. It was a cloudless night, the stars glittering brightly in the heavens, a dazzling cape thrown across the shoulders of the night. The quarter-moon moved silently through the darkness, casting its pearl luminescence over the earth below. Content as never before, Storm rested her head on Bram's shoulder as they drank in the miracle of life surrounding them. She had changed into a pair of jeans, an apricot sweater, and a lightweight white-canvas jacket with blue piping. A slight offshore breeze brought the tangy scent of salt with it, and she inhaled it deeply.

"I feel like the ocean tonight," she admitted softly to Bram, "moody, restless, changing . . ."

Bram tightened his arm around her waist momentarily. "You're allowed. Happy?"

Storm nodded. "Very. You?"

"The same."

A smile tinged her lips as she glanced up at him. "Talkative bunch, aren't we? Everything we feel or sense can be boiled down to one or two syllables."

His mouth curved upward as he watched Storm, pulling her to a halt and turning her around to face him. "Okay, what gives?" he asked, resting his hands on her shoulders.

"Nothing. I'm just happy."

Bram leaned down, placing a kiss on her parted lips. "Talk to me," he coaxed against her mouth. "What's going on inside that head of yours? I can see it in your eyes."

She laughed softly. "Remember that time I called you an insensitive rock?"

"Yeah, that and a few other choice expletives," he remarked wryly.

"Well, I was wrong. You aren't, Bram." Storm's eyes grew tender. "Just the opposite really. The last two months I've started to realize how sensitive you are."

He shrugged, giving her a teasing look. "It's your fault, you know," he drawled.

Storm tilted her head, not sure whether he was serious or still teasing her. Her mouth set into a petulant line. "Bram Gallagher, why do you always get silly when I'm trying to be serious?"

"I'm sorry, princess. You're so much fun to tease. You're the straight person on our team and I'm the comic. I love playing off your serious side. Am I forgiven?"

Her gray eyes danced with laughter while she tried to suppress a growing smile. "I don't think you'll ever get rid of that fighter-jock sense of humor."

"Ever want me to?"

"Never. You make me laugh when things get bad."

He ran his hands down her arms. "I know. But we're a good balance for one another. I crack jokes to relieve the tension, and you sit there with your unreadable face, eyes narrowed and lips set. We just have different ways of dealing with stress."

"It's a good thing one of us is serious, or we'd be called the Laurel and Hardy of the air station."

Bram raised an eyebrow at her. "Oh? Am I known as the clown of our fine team efforts?"

Storm chortled, falling back into his arms, savoring

his closeness. "You know the guys respect you." Reaching up, she caressed his cheek. "You've added a new dimension to all of our lives, Bram. And we're the better for it."

His eyes became softer as he observed her. "You've added a few new dimensions to my life, lady, in case you hadn't realized it."

"Yeah?"

"Yeah."

"Like how?"

He raised his chin. "Oh, in many small but important ways."

Storm's smile died on her lips as she regarded him in the gathering silence. "Tell me how I've touched you, Bram," she whispered.

Resting his jaw against her hair, he held her tightly within his embrace. "You've taught me a lot about women, Storm. When I first met you, I thought you were going to be one tough broad to deal with, but I was wrong. It was your ability to say Hey, I'm just an average human being doing a job I love to do. No big deal. I don't have to be macho to fly helicopters. I don't have to prove a thing to any man." He kissed her temple. "Normally women in a heavily male-occupied field tend to get defensive and put up all kinds of walls to protect themselves emotionally."

She nuzzled against the rough weave of the jacket he wore, seeking his warmth. "But I didn't have to, Bram. The Coast Guard's attitude toward women working in supposedly male occupations is vastly different from the other services. Here you're a part of a larger team. A loose-knit family concept."

"Still," he insisted, "you could have been tough with me because of the way I behaved at first. But you weren't. You just persevered, restrained yourself, and let me get all the kinks out of my system." He sobered more. "I was deeply touched by your ability to display your emotions, Storm. On and off the job. I came to realize that when you cried in front of a bunch of pilots or crewpeople, it didn't lessen their respect for you in any way. By your being human, you allowed all of us to let down our barriers and express our feelings more openly too."

She tipped her head, meeting his troubled gaze. "I think one of the worst things that has happened to us in the last decade as men and women is that displaying our emotions was considered wrong or weak." She gave a doleful shake of her head. "Bram, we never get rid of what we feel inside. I find it infinitely easier to show my vulnerability than to hide it and pretend it doesn't exist."

"But when you show your emotions, it makes me feel like it's all right to show mine." He groped for the right words. "I guess I've learned from you that if you are vulnerable, the other person isn't likely to hurt you."

She nodded. "Show your underbelly and your enemy will slit it open, right?"

"Right. Maggie was like that. She never shared that other side of herself with me. I knew it was there; I felt it, and sometimes I heard it in her voice. But she never trusted me enough with her feelings." He kissed her cheek. "On the other hand, you literally placed yourself in my hands from the day we met. You made no excuses for your feelings, and at first, I found that frightening because I had no idea *what* to do with them or you."

"We had a few stops and starts, Bram, but you've been wonderful."

One corner of his mouth lifted. "Sometimes I feel like a first-class klutz with you, Storm. You know who you are. You know what's right and wrong for you. It's that invisible stability around you that I sense, and see operating on a twenty-four-hour basis. I just shake my head wondering how in the hell you got so together before age thirty."

She shared his smile. "You mean you don't have to be over the hill in order to have developed some maturity?"

Bram ran his hand lightly across her hair, smoothing strands away from her cheek. "I'm thirty-two and I still haven't gotten it together, Storm."

"Yes, you have, Bram. In many ways. Look, I'm not perfect. Far from it. Maybe I reflect an area of weakness that you have right now. But you're aware that being vulnerable isn't all that painful, and you're working on it."

He slid his hands down her back, coming to rest against her hips, rocking her gently in his arms. "You are perfect."

"I am not!"

Laughing, he enjoyed watching the play of emotions across her mobile features. "Tell me where you aren't, then," he challenged teasingly.

Her heart took a painful, aching leap in her chest. She wet her lips, allowing the fear she felt to dissipate beneath his cobalt eyes. "I'm afraid to live, Bram," she admitted thickly.

"What?" He snorted. "That's not true. I don't know what you call it when you hang your rear out the line with these SAR missions. Or experience the pain of losing a survivor. You don't run away from life. You couldn't, and do the job we do."

Sliding her fingers up across his chest, she allowed them to come to rest near his shoulders. "I'm saying it the wrong way." Her voice dropped into a softened whisper. "Do you remember the time you volunteered to stay aboard the *Antonia*?"

Bram sensed the change in her and became serious. "Haven't ever forgotten it, Storm. Why?"

Her fingers curved into the material of his jacket and she fearlessly met his questioning eyes. "When we rescued you later, do you remember how upset I was?"

"Yes. But when things are tense, you're always like that, whether I'm involved in it or not."

That was true. Her gray eyes turned bleak. "I found out that day just how much you meant to me, Bram." Her voice broke. "I was afraid. More than I could ever recall in my life."

Gently he cupped her chin. "Maybe because you cared a little for me?"

Her eyes sparkled with unshed tears. "Maybe . . ."

Bram studied her in the interim silence, his sensual mouth compressing. "I think what I'm hearing you say, Storm, is that you're afraid to get totally involved with me emotionally. Is that it? You're afraid to live on the razor edge of a commitment again?"

Tears made shimmering paths down her drawn cheeks. "Y-yes . . ."

He inhaled, deeply touched by her honesty. "I'm not exactly a safe bet," he admitted ruefully. "I'm divorced, and searching around for parts and pieces of myself that I hadn't been aware of before you crashed into my life." His features mellowed. "Tonight, Storm, I watched you as we walked around talking with the guys and their wives. I love watching your mobile expressions, your clear, uninhibited laughter, your ability to reach out and touch others. And I found myself wanting you all to myself. I just wanted to grab your hand, run out the door, and take you here to the beach."

Storm closed her eyes. "I'm afraid, Bram . . . afraid that if—if I allow myself to love you like I want, that—that you'll be torn away from me like Hal was. . . ."

"Oh, honey," he murmured thickly, embracing her. He felt her tremble and realized she was crying. His heart wrenched in his chest, and he began to stroke her hair. "Nothing's going to happen to me. I'm too damn mean to die. Heaven certainly doesn't want to punch my ticket yet, and the devil sure as hell doesn't want me either," he playfully teased, "so you're stuck with me."

She gripped the material of his jacket, allowing all her pent-up fears over the last few months to surface. Bram's voice was a soothing balm to her ravaged emotional state.

"And speaking of love, Storm," he reminded her gently, raising her chin so he could meet her eyes, "I have a confession of my own to make. Ever since that day on the *Antonia*, I realized that I loved you." He grimaced, looking up into the night. "And I was just as afraid for different reasons to tell you how I felt." Bram gave a shake of his head, again searching her face. "Now that I've said it, it wasn't so hard after all." He smiled tenderly as he framed her face with his hands. "I think I'll say it again because it felt so good: I love you, Storm Travis. Now that you know that, what are you going to do with that little piece of information?"

Storm uttered a small cry of joy, flinging her arms around his neck. "Oh, Bram," she softly sobbed, "I love you too . . ."

He chuckled. "Well, don't sound so happy about it."

Their laughter intermingled with the crashing surf, and Bram lifted her off her feet, turning her around in a circle until both of them were so dizzy they lost their balance and fell into an unceremonious heap into each other's arms. Bram cushioned their fall, twisting so that he hit the hard sand first to protect Storm. He grinned, rolling her to his side; holding her; kissing her eyes, nose, and mouth with quick warm kisses. Storm giggled, struggling to sit up but he wouldn't let her.

"Oh, no," he breathed, "you're going nowhere, my lady." He proffered his arm as a pillow for her head, laying above her until she stopped giggling. Her eyes were shining with happiness; her lips were parted, curving into a wonderful smile. "I don't know what's so funny about me admitting I love you, Travis," he said, a bit breathless from all their exertion.

"You're crazy, Gallagher!" she protested, running her slender fingers through his dark hair.

"But you love me anyway?"

"Yes," she admitted huskily, "I love you anyway."

"Still afraid?"

She gave a grave nod of her head.

Bram smiled. "Good. So am I. We'll be scared together, okay?"

"Okay . . ."

"Misery loves company, you know."

"Trite but true," Storm conceded, loving his warmth, his ability to be emotionally honest with her.

He raised his head, a euphoric smile on his face. "If this is misery, then I'm going to love every second of it with you."

"Does anything ever faze you?" she asked wonderingly as Bram helped her stand. He brushed the sand from her back and rear, enjoying his duty.

"Yes. You did. You walked into my well-ordered life and blew it all to hell. That's what you did, Travis." He gave her a wicked glint, placing his arms around her shoulder and drawing her near as they began the long walk back to the car.

"Poor baby," she taunted. "I suppose you want an air medal for bravery, hanging in there with me through our ups and downs."

"No, but a Purple Heart would be in keeping."

Storm gasped and hit him playfully on the arm. "Purple Heart! When did I ever wound anything more than that swelled-headed ego of yours, Gallagher?"

He tried to appear hurt. "Ugh! The lady has just wounded me in action again!" He threw his hand across his chest, pretending injury.

"Straighten up and fly right, lieutenant," she told him, a glimmer of laughter in her eyes.

Bram feigned hurt. "You'd think an ex–fighter jock would get a fair shake with you, lieutenant. But I can tell you don't love me. . . ."

She smiled. "Just wait until we get home," she urged. "Then you'll find out just how much I love you, ex–fighter jock."

"Yeah?"

"Yeah."

A softened smile touched his mouth as he kissed her hair. "Merry Christmas, princess. I couldn't have gotten a better present than those three words from your lovely lips and beautiful heart."

Storm gave him a warm look. "Merry Christmas, Bram. I've never had a happier one, believe me."

"I believe you," he whispered, losing his smile. "This coming year will be a new chapter in both of our lives," he promised her. "And I can't think of a finer gift than giving our love to one another. Come on; let's get home. We've got two days together, and I don't want to waste one precious second of it."

Christmas morning dawned brightly with the sun burning off the low hanging clouds that had moved inland from the ocean overnight. Storm lingered with Bram over coffee in the sunlit living room. Her body tingled pleasantly from recent lovemaking and she eyed him lovingly. His arm rested around her shoulders as she leaned against him.

"Merry Christmas," she whispered.

Bram's face reflected his unspoken affection. "The best ever, princess."

A knock at the front door startled them both. Storm frowned, setting the cup down on the coffee table.

"You expecting anyone?" Bram asked.

"No . . ."

Bram watched her move across the living room to answer the insistent knock. Even in a pale pink blouse and jeans she looked incredibly feminine, and his body tightened with desire for her again. Storm opened the door and he heard her gasp.

"Matt! What—"

"May I come in, Storm?"

Her eyes widened and she stepped aside for her brother. "Of course."

Bram rose, watching as Storm threw her arms around a dark-haired man who easily matched his own six-feet-one-inch height. Storm sobbed as she clung to the stranger. Bram walked toward them and waited until they parted.

"Oh, Matt," Storm whispered. "It's been so long since—my God, I'm glad to see you." Then she realized Bram was standing nearby. Trying to wipe the sudden tears that had appeared on her cheeks, she smiled tremulously up at him.

"Bram, I want you to meet my youngest brother, Matt Travis. Matt, this is Bram Gallagher."

Bram extended his hand. "A pleasure," he declared.

Like an excited little girl, Storm placed her hands on her cheeks for just a moment. "Come in, Matt. Have you had breakfast yet?"

He shook his head as Storm led him through the foyer. Wearing a rumpled well-traveled dark suit, he pulled off his coat, allowing it to hang over the back of the couch. "No. I just hopped a flight from D.C. to come down here. Can't stand airline food."

Worriedly Storm searched her brother's face. He looked exhausted, shadows skirting his gray eyes. Matt had always been the best-looking of the three siblings, but now his handsome face was drawn and pale. Taking his arm, she propelled him toward the bathroom.

"You also haven't shaved. Look, you're beat. Did you just get off an assignment?"

Matt ran his fingers through his dark brown hair. "Yeah. I haven't eaten or slept in almost two days."

Bram leaned against the kitchen doorway, hands stuffed in his pockets, watching Storm take command. A smile lingered at the corners of his mouth. She fussed over Matt like a mother—her voice was low and coaxing as she kept a hand on her brother's broad slumped shoulder and led him into the bedroom. It looked like more coffee was in order, and he roused himself, moving to the kitchen to prepare a fresh pot.

Storm joined him ten minutes later, her brow furrowed. Bram took her into his arms.

"You all right?" he inquired, concerned.

She closed her eyes, leaning against Bram's solid chest, his heartbeat soothing her disordered emotional state. "Yes and no," she replied. "My God, I never expected to see Matt."

"Does he always drop in like this?" he asked wryly.

Storm shook her head. "I told you a little bit about Cal, my older brother. He's the jet jockey in the Marine Corps." Her eyes glimmered as she studied Bram's face. "He's a lot like you—brash, brazen, arrogant—"

He grinned. "Okay, I get the picture. And Matt?"

Rubbing her forehead, Storm stepped out of the protective haven of Bram's arms and wandered aimlessly about the kitchen, finally sitting down at the table. "Matt's the youngest. He's twenty-seven." She frowned. "He's an FBI agent, Bram. A year ago his wife was killed by Juan Garcia, a drug smuggler who runs a powerful ring in Colombia and the U.S. Matt had been working as an undercover agent here in Florida, and when Garcia learned that he was responsible for putting some of his top men in prison, he put out a contract on Matt's wife."

Bram scowled, joining her at the table. "Damn, that's a tough nut to swallow. I'm sorry, Storm."

"It happened six months before I met you," she began softly, her eyes silver with unshed tears. "Matt was the quietest of the three of us. As brash and outspoken as Cal and I are, Matt just keeps everything inside. And when his wife, Maura, was killed in an unexplained 'auto accident,' Matt lost it." She rubbed her face, staring over at Bram. "He's living life with a vengeance in order to get at the mobster who set the wheels in motion to kill her. Since Maura's death, he's been undercover. I've rarely seen him or been in contact with him." She chewed on her lower lip. "God, he's lost so much weight. He looks terrible."

Bram reached out and gripped her hand. "Is there anything we can do to help him?"

Tears slipped down her cheeks as she met his concerned gaze. "Do you know how much I love you for asking that?" she confided.

His grip on her hand tightened slightly. "Family means a lot to me, Storm. Just like it does to you. He's your brother and I can tell you love him an awful lot."

She wanted to get up and throw her arms around him and simply hold him. "Matt's here for a reason. He said he's got a few days off before the action begins. If I can get a couple of decent meals into him and get him to sleep, I think that's all we can do for him right now."

"He's a man on the run, Storm," he told her quietly. "I recognize the look in his eyes. I used to look like that myself when Maggie wanted to call it quits." His expression grew warm. "But I'm not running anymore. I found a woman who I can love without reservation. Maybe when Matt finds someone else, he'll quit running too."

Storm agreed. "God, when Maura died, Matt came unglued. Both Cal and I flew up to Clearwater, where it happened. It was the worst nightmare of my life except for Hal's death."

Bram got up and poured them each a fresh cup of coffee and then sat back down beside her. "Matt's here on an undercover assignment?"

Storm nodded and got up to putter around the kitchen, putting bacon in a skillet to fry. "He mumbled something about working with the Coasties on busting part of Garcia's drug-smuggling operation in the Bahamas this time. He'll probably fly out of here and go down there in a day or two." She shook her head, setting a plate and silverware on the table. "I hate the thought of it."

Bram grimaced. "I don't mind working with the other agencies on a combined operation, but everyone's got guns except us. We're sitting ducks up in the cockpit of a 52."

Storm agreed. Getting shot at wasn't her idea of Coast Guard flying. The pilots sitting in the helicopters were clear, unobstructed targets. Not only that, but the fuel rested in the bottom of the 52. One bullet through the tank, and they would explode into flames. Bram had been with her on two combined operations to net drug smugglers at sea, and each time he had snarled something about at least getting a damn bulletproof vest to wear on these missions.

Matt appeared a half-hour later, freshly showered, his skin now scraped free of a day's worth of beard. His lean face seemed almost gaunt in appearance. Bram invited him to sit down and handed him a hot cup of coffee. Storm placed a plate heaped with three eggs, six strips of bacon, plus a steaming hefty portion of home fries before him. Matt gave his sister a warm look, and the first smile they had seen on his wide expressive mouth.

"Obviously you think I need to eat, sis."

Storm put her hands on her hips. "No arguments, Matt. You're skinny as hell."

"That's my sister for you," Matt confided to Bram, a gleam of affection in his charcoal eyes.

"She's that way with everybody," Bram assured him, grinning at Storm.

"Now, don't you two think you can gang up on me," she warned both of them, sitting down.

Matt dug hungrily into the homemade food. "Somehow, Storm, you'll keep us in line."

Bram gave her a fond glance. "I can testify to that."

"Keep it up, guys. I'm warning you . . ."

Storm studied her brother as he ate. She tried to hide her shock over Matt's condition. He wasn't heavily built like Bram; his body was much leaner and tightly muscled. Now his one-hundred-eighty-pound weight had slipped to less than one-sixty. She noticed that the blue shirt and jeans he wore hung loosely on his body. And his eyes were not only ringed with exhaustion, but bloodshot as well. "What have they been doing, working you to death, Matt?"

He shrugged and reached for a jar of jam. "We're getting closer to busting Garcia. It's taken me a year to set this up, but now it looks like we're going to be able to cut into his operation by about forty percent." Matt looked up, a pleased expression on his normally unreadable features. "And that will force the bastard back to the gulf and the Texas connection, where we can pin him down. This is step two we'll be initiating now." He spread some jam on the whole wheat toast. "That's why I decided to drop in on you. According to the operation's plans, two helicopter crews from the Miami Coast Guard air station will fly down to the Bahamas to work with us. We finally got permission from the Bahamian government to do it."

Storm's brows rose and she shifted to observe Bram. "Oh? It must be a big bust."

Matt viewed her and then Bram before he resumed eating. "I've already seen the orders. You and Bram are one of the crews going down with us."

Bram scowled. "There's a good chance of gunplay."

"You'd better believe it." He gave a doleful shake of his head. "As soon as I found out you were assigned, Storm, I tried to influence my superiors to get you off the schedule. But apparently your skills are too good to pass up, and they wanted the two top crews from the Miami station in on this." He reached over and took her hand. "I don't think women should be around an operation of this kind. It's just too damned dangerous."

Bram got up, his mouth compressed into a single line. He walked around the kitchen, hands resting tensely on his hips. There was no way in hell he wanted Storm in on that operation. He groped for a way to keep her off the forthcoming bust.

"Isn't there some kind of regulation that says the military can't have two members from the same family in a combat zone at the same time?" he queried.

Matt looked up, taking a sip of his coffee. "That's a good argument and would hold water except that I'm working in a civilian agency function and am not considered military. The FBI interfaces with the military in regard to drug smugglers all the time. I've already tried that approach, Bram, and it went over like a lead balloon." He stole a look at Storm's placid features. It never ceased to amaze him how stable she was, regardless of the situation. "Sis, this is one time I wish you weren't so damn good at flying helicopters."

9

~ooooooooo~

Bram sat gloomily opposite Storm as Captain Greer waited for Lieutenant Kyle Armstrong and his copilot to enter the briefing room. It was one hell of a post–Christmas present, Bram thought, disgruntled. Present in the room besides the Coast Guard pilots and cutter skippers were three FBI agents, Matt Travis among them, and a few Customs and Drug Enforcement Agency agents. They sat stoically at the oblong mahogany table with their cups of coffee in hand. The bright-orange flight suits of the Coast Guard pilots stood out in sharp contrast to the conservative suits worn by the other agents. An older man of fifty had eyed Storm keenly when she had first walked into the room. Bram hoped the agent would protest her taking part in the bust and get her reassigned.

He hadn't slept well last night. Wasn't Storm worried that she could be killed? She had slept soundly in his arms, head nestled beneath his chin, her free arm and leg thrown across his body. And he had stared up at the ceiling and listened to the clock tick with its phosphorescent red figures glowing in the darkness. He loved Storm fiercely. He didn't want to lose her.

Bram moodily stared down at his half-empty coffeecup. Matt Travis was a shell of a man living inside a body, running away from the grief and loss of his wife. A cold fear snaked through Bram. He'd be the same way if anything ever happened to Storm and he knew it. Suddenly life became precious drops of golden moments with her. Bram swallowed against the anxiety he felt winding its way up to form a lump in his throat. As he stared across the table at Storm, he realized the full impact of just how much he loved her. Matt Travis's sudden appearance into their lives had effectively ripped away any ghostly doubts as to how he felt. Life had taken a perverse turn, and he didn't like it at all. Bram wanted the time to continue cultivating their ever-deepening relationship. And he knew Storm felt similarly. The days and nights they were able to spend in each other's arms were precious and far between, but it kept them going. It kept them anticipating the next time they could share a day off together. Bram glared at Commander Harrison, who had approved the roster of crews to fly for the operation. Storm would be flying into danger. What the hell could he do about it? Nothing, a desperate voice declared inside him. Not a damn thing.

"I believe everyone is present," Commander Harrison averred, shutting the door. He looked over at the FBI agent. "Inspector Preston, you may start your presentation."

Preston was a slender man with long bony hands. He shut off the lights and turned on the projector. "For the past two-and-a-half years we've been infiltrating Juan Garcia's Colombian operation. He peddles mainly coke and grass to the Texas gulf and Florida peninsula. Although Garcia is Colombian, he owns a large estate on Andros Island in the Bahamas, where much of the coke is stored before it is airlifted or dropped by ship along our coast." He flashed a picture of an island clothed in forests of Australian pine, palms, and a chain of hills that looked like welts in the fabric of the pancake-flat island.

"This is Andros Island. It is situated west of Nassau. Andros is an ideal center for Garcia because it's less popular with tourists and to a certain degree offers natural barriers to prevent us from spying. The island is littered with skeletons of planes carrying drugs that crashed there. We've gotten word through our undercover man that Garcia is planning to send a mother ship loaded with grass and coke out to meet with smaller boats." He pointed to a crescent-shaped bay sporting a small strip of white sand, protected by a group of hills overlooking the bay. "He's going to anchor in Chisholm Bay and hoist the drugs over the side to waiting boat customers. Commander Harrison?"

Bram's scowl deepened, but he remained silent. The hooked curve of the bay didn't seem to allow much room to safely maneuver many ships. He cast a glance over at two SES cutter skippers who were also in attendance.

"Thank you, Inspector. The Coast Guard's part in this multiarmed operation is twofold. First we will provide two H-52 helicopters to pick up the combined FBI and Customs teams and drop them on Garcia's mother ship, *La Ceiba*. Then the SES cutters *Osprey* and *Sea Hawk* will close the noose from the sea and shut off any escape attempt out of Chisholm. No craft will be allowed to get by the SES contingent." Harrison looked pleased. "In other words, we're sealing off their only route of escape. They have nowhere to go and will have to surrender."

Storm cast a horrified look over at Matt, who appeared composed and unaffected by the plan. They would drop five men onto the deck of an unfriendly ship? Smugglers always carried a wide array of weapons. The chances of the agents getting wounded or killed would be high! Her throat ached with tears; she felt terror for Matt. He had been through one of the most brutal years of his life, but this was no way to end it! Did he want to die because he had loved Maura so much? Her stomach knotted and reflexively Storm lifted her chin, seeking Bram's reassuring gaze.

Bram saw the silent terror mirrored in Storm's eyes. He grimly turned the coffee mug around and around in his hands.

After everyone had received detailed information about Operation Stingray, the commander looked down the table. "Are there any questions?"

Bram circumspectly eased out of his slouched position. "What kind of resistance are you expecting aboard the *La Ceiba*, Inspector?"

"Minimal, Lieutenant Gallagher. We feel that the element of surprise will reduce the chance of our teams or your helicopters taking any fire. Most mother ships are used to boardings by the SES cutter crews. We intend to expand the use of your CG helicopters to assume a larger role in catching smugglers. We realize this mission is setting a precedent, and we have no statistics to report our findings yet. Commander Harrison has picked the best crews for this job, and we have every confidence in your skills." He smiled.

Bram didn't. "Look, I know this is an extremely unusual situation, but women in any other service are banned from taking part in combat." His eyes narrowed on Harrison. "And where we're going, it *is* going to be combat."

Harrison gave a curt nod of his head, his focus latching onto Storm. "Ordinarily you're right, Lieutenant Gallagher. But the Coast Guard is caught in a catch-22. We have women serving in both the enlisted and officers' ranks aboard cutters constantly prowling the ocean for drug smugglers. They carry weapons just like any other member of a boarding crew. As long as a war is not declared, our women have to take their chances right alongside the men of the Coast Guard. If war were declared, then the U.S. Navy would have to decide whether the women should remain in combat positions or not. I realize your concern, Lieutenant Gallagher, but Lieutenant Travis happens to be the best when it comes to flying in tight situations. You might as well know she was my first choice."

Bram checked his anger and frustration, lapsing back into silence, but continued to glower at the commander. "I assume since we're going into a combat situation, the 52 crews will get some sort of protection?" he inquired icily.

"Bulletproof vests will be issued before you lift off from Nassau."

"No .45s or .38s?" Bram asked, disbelief in his voice.

Commander Harrison shook his head. "We didn't feel there was a need, quite frankly. Up to now, no CG helicopter has been fired on, and we presume this procedure will continue." He shrugged. "Let's face it, the drug smugglers caught by the Coast Guard will get two years in prison. If they shoot at or kill one of you, the courts will keep them for twenty-five years. They aren't stupid. We feel the smugglers will continue to hold off from firing on Coast Guard personnel. All you have to do is hover, drop the teams, and loiter around until you're told to land back on Andros. Also we'll need you to take the teams back to Nassau along with the high-level prisoners we hope to capture on this trip after the situation is secured."

Bram hunched forward, both hands on the table. "Frankly, sir, when everyone else is provided weapons, I'd think it would be a blanket policy that we're at least issued shoulder holsters. Just in case."

The room crackled with tension. Storm stole a look over at Kyle Armstrong. It was obvious that he wanted a weapon too. Nervously she knitted her fingers in her lap beneath the table, remaining silent.

Harrison's patience was threadbare. "I'll take that suggestion under advisement, Lieutenant Gallagher. If the policy changes, you'll know about it before you fly over. Any other questions? Very well; dismissed. The 52 crews have the rest of the day off. Be here at 1800 to fly to Nassau."

Bram remained ominously silent as Storm walked at his side. They left the Administration building, heading toward her sports car in the parking lot. The sun was shining brightly, the humidity rising with the temperature.

Once inside the car, Storm turned to him. "Let's do something special today, Bram," she begged him. "For us."

His heart contracted as he heard the tremor in her voice. "You feel it too?"

"What?"

"I've got a bad feeling about this one, Storm."

Reaching over, she slid her hand down his arm, entwining her fingers within his. "I know it's hard on you, Bram."

His mouth quirked as if he were experiencing pain. "Hard? Scared would be more accurate. Scared of losing you on some asinine operation where they won't even give us minimal protection in case we need it." Frustration laced his tone, and he shook his head. "I've never felt this helpless before."

"It'll be okay," she reassured him. "Come on; want to go to the beach? Our favorite spot? We don't have to be back here for eight hours." Her gray eyes turned pewter with silent pleading. "Say yes."

Bram lifted her hand to his lips, kissing her palm. "Let's go."

Bram lay moodily on the blanket and watched Storm run into the waves, diving into the turquoise ocean and swimming strongly beyond the breakers. He lay on his side, hand propped against his head, allowing the late-December sunlight to warm him. The beach was crowded as usual for this time of year, but all his attention remained focused on Storm. She was so full of life. Closing his eyes, he pictured her smiling face with those haunting gray eyes glimmering with joy. Grimacing, he turned on his belly. What the hell was he going to do? It was impossible to fight City Hall. He couldn't disobey orders. Even Matt Travis couldn't swing enough weight to get Storm removed from the operation.

Storm jogged back up to the blanket, her body shimmering with droplets of water. Flinging herself down beside Bram, she laughed throatily, sliding her arm around his broad shoulders and placing a wet kiss on his cheek.

"Come on! The water's wonderful, Bram."

He forced a smile. Her dark hair was wet and glistening, her full mouth drawn into a teasing grin, her slender body beautifully outlined by the green suit she wore. "All I want is you," he murmured.

Wiping her face, she plopped herself down, beaming. "You've got me, jet jockey."

"Not like I want."

Storm tilted her head, a gleam in her eye. "I'm afraid the beach is a little too crowded for what you have in mind."

He grinned. She was right—she made his body harden with desire for her. No matter whether she wore a flight suit, civilian clothes, or nothing at all, she was desirable to him. "Come here, wet puppy; I want to talk seriously with you." He reached out, pulling her forward so she fell gracefully beside him. Smoothing several locks of hair still beaded with water from her brow, he leaned over, capturing her smiling lips. Her mouth was warm and salty-tasting, supple and pliant beneath his demands. She pressed herself suggestively against his length, and he groaned.

"You could turn a rock on," he grumbled.

Laughing, Storm traced the solid line of his jaw with her fingertips. "Just you, I hope."

"Always, princess."

Closing her eyes for a moment, she whispered, "I'm so glad we came out here today, Bram. Thank you."

He lost his smile, the blue of his eyes intensifying. "You are a wonderful woman," he declared. "So easy to please . . ."

"It doesn't take much to make me happy," she agreed, reopening her eyes and responding to the caress of his eyes. "The whole family was bred to the bone on the simple pleasures of life."

"Such as?"

"Oh, just a few innocent notions—like happiness is obtainable. Something that everyone in the world is searching for all their lives." Mirth glimmered in her eyes. "And love. Our family believed that both could be found."

"Two of the most prized, sought-after possessions in the universe," Bram added, caressing her cheek. "Your parents are either idealists or dreamers."

She turned, kissing him delicately on his sensitive palm, watching the effect on him. "One of these days you'll meet my parents. And you'll discover that they're pretty squared away. Not pie-in-the-sky dreamers who filled their children's heads full of the impossible."

"You found happiness and love with Hal," he offered.

Storm became more sober. "Yes, yes, I did." She lifted her lashes, meeting his burning azure gaze that sent a tingle of longing through her. "But I've found happiness and love a second time too." She ran her tongue across her lower lip. "With you, Bram."

He brought her into the shelter of his embrace, and she rested her head on his forearm, staring up at him. Her ginger hair was beginning to dry, a few strands lifting in the gentle sea breeze. Her face was a golden tan, her cheeks stained with a faint pink flush of exertion. She looked ageless—so much a child and yet a mature woman who intimately knew herself. He caught those rebellious tresses from her cheek, tucking them behind one ear.

"Marry me, Storm."

Her dove-gray eyes widened. "What?"

He regarded her steadily. "Marry me."

A look of confusion blended with hesitation as she stared up at him. "You serious? Or is this one of your little jokes?"

Bram muttered something under his breath and rolled his eyes. "A joke? How often do you think I go around asking women to marry me? After my track record? A joke! . . . Well, I'll be damned."

"Then, you're serious!"

Bram gave her an exasperated look. "Of course I am."

Storm eyed him suspiciously, laughter lurking in the depths of her eyes. "This isn't some masterminded plan of yours to get me taken off that operation, is it?"

Bram uttered another expletive, pulling her up so they sat cross-legged opposite each other, holding her hands. "I'm trying to be serious, Storm."

"Then, you shouldn't be teasing me all the time so I think everything you ask is a joke, Bram Gallagher!"

"Okay, okay." He tried to compose himself. "First you accuse me of playing a joke on you and then of being sneaky enough to get you off that operation. Do you always think I have ulterior motives?"

Storm grinned broadly. "You usually do."

"I had that coming."

"And marrying me? Is there a method to your madness in getting me to be your wife?" she teased saucily.

Bram held her hands within his, sobering. "I sat in that conference room this morning, Storm, and I got scared. Scared like I've never been before. I sat there realizing that if something happened to you, I'd end up like your brother Matt. Lost, lonely, and bitter." His voice became husky as he saw Storm's features grow vulnerable with his admission. "I don't know what Hal was like. I have a feeling he was an easygoing man, compared to me. I do know that if you marry me, we'll have our moments where the sparks will really fly because we're both very headstrong, opinionated people. But we also have the maturity and respect for each other to weather those periods." His azure eyes grew warm. "I've been thinking about asking you to marry me for quite a while, Storm. But I was afraid. Afraid that I'd somehow botch up our chances, and I didn't want to do that. You deserve the very best I can be, and I felt I was still trying to get parts and pieces of me put back together again."

"Oh, Bram—"

"Shh," he admonished gently. "Let me get all of this off my chest and then you can talk." His brow furrowed, and he gazed at her long slender fingers. She was an artist in so many ways, he thought. "Over the last five months, you've taught me that not all women are afraid to entrust themselves to a man's care." He shrugged. "You trusted me. And because of that, I've opened up with you. I've found life's been pretty decent since doing that. I like giving and sharing myself with you and vice versa, I believe."

Storm waited a moment. Her eyes grew misty with tears as she said softly, "It was easy to place myself in your hands, Bram. Don't ask me how I knew I'd be safe doing it, I only knew I would be. And you've never taken advantage of me. When two people bare their souls to one another, it has to be one of the greatest compliments to themselves and to each other. It means not only trust between them, but as you said, respecting each other's feelings."

He kissed each of her hands. "You've shown me a lot, princess."

"You gave me back my will to live again, Bram."

"Then, spend the rest of your life with me, Storm."

Tears streaked her cheeks as she met his suspiciously bright blue eyes. "Think you can put up with my moodiness?"

"You're like the ocean—quicksilver. I love that about you. I'll never come home to the same woman two nights in a row."

She laughed gently. "You must be a glutton for punishment, then."

"No, I just prefer a woman with diamondlike facets." He slid his hand behind her neck, pulling her slightly forward, his mouth caressing her lips. "I want to spend the rest of my life discovering all the facets of you, Storm."

She pressed her lips to his, relishing his strength, his tenderness. "Discover me," she urged against his mouth.

By three P.M. they were back at Storm's house. Bram took the beach bag from her, setting it aside as they entered.

"Come on," he said, "let's take a shower together."

Storm looked up at him, her heart pounding erratically. On the beach, she had wanted simply to fall into his arms and love him wholly, completely. "Yes," she murmured, taking his hand, allowing him to lead. She ached to be one with him, to seal the love between them on all levels, not just emotionally and mentally. Fear lurked in the recesses of Bram's eyes, and she sensed his silent anguish over the forthcoming operation. He was afraid of losing her. Although she tried not to let it show, Storm had to admit that she was afraid of losing him as well.

"Come here," he entreated, turning her toward him. Slipping his hands beneath the straps of the bathing suit, he eased them away from her shoulders. His calloused hands slid downward, gently cupping her taut breasts, and he ran his palms across her hardening nipples.

A small gasp escaped from Storm as she shivered beneath his skillful, provocative touch. The sultry steam rose from the shower as they removed their suits and entered it. The hot water pummeled her body, and Storm closed her eyes, allowing the rivulets to cleanse her hair. Bram picked up the bar of soap in his large hands, running it slowly, arousingly across her shoulders, breasts, and abdomen. She tingled beneath his touch, the water and soap creating even more delightful friction. Turning her around, he lathered her beautifully curved back and hips, and down her long coltish legs. A soft moan slid from her throat, and she turned, placing her arms around his shoulders.

"My turn," she said huskily, kissing his mouth with small teasing nips. She felt his hardness pressing against her lower body and drank hungrily of the taste of his mouth. She was quivering against him, wanting him, needing him. Her fingers moved across the breadth of his chest, the soap a liquid pleasure creating even more tactile sensations than she thought possible. Storm watched him through half-closed eyes as she allowed her hands to trail down across his flat belly to the carpet of thick wiry hair below. He groaned, the sound reverberating in the enclosed space. His mouth plundered her yielding lips, drinking deeply of her as he slipped his hands downward, capturing her waist. Warm water trickled across them in tantalizing streams, further goading them toward unrestrained passion.

Leaning over, he ran his tongue across her nipples, feeling her knees buckle, her body bending like a willow against him. A soaring joy engulfed him as he realized she was easily fulfilled by him. He sucked gently on her taut, hardened nipples; heard her chant his name again and again, her fingers digging convulsively into his shoulders. Lifting his head, he kissed her mouth, branding her as his alone, forever. In one smooth motion, he brought her upward against him, allowing her to slide downward, capturing him with her warm, welcoming body. She froze in ecstasy, her head thrown back, a cry of pleasure escaping her lips. Blood pounded through his aching, hard body, and he trembled with the knowledge that they loved each other with a fierceness that left them both breathless in its wake.

Her lashes lifted, revealing languorous gray eyes silvered with hunger and intensity as Storm felt his need within her inviting body. The steam curled around and between them, the tiny fingers of water adding tiny jolts of pleasure for each of them. Together they drove each other over the edge of oblivion. Moments later Storm rested her head against Bram's shoulder, fulfilled as never before. A low groan from deep within his body had told her that he, too, had found the ultimate release within her—the gift of the love shared between them.

Bram eased her from the shower, wrapped her in a thick luxurious towel, and then picked her up. She clung weakly to him, her head nestled against his shoulder as he carried her into the bedroom. Sunlight filtered through the lace curtains, giving the room a muted glow that matched their mood. Placing her on the bed, Bram drew Storm into his arms, gently kissing her swollen lips. Her hair was dark and wet, and he smoothed it from her cheek and brow.

"I love you," he told her, watching her lashes move upward, revealing breathtaking gray eyes that shone with returned love.

"Oh, Bram," she said shakily, leaning upward to kiss him reverently.

He drew her close, holding her, feeling the strong beat of her heart against his chest. Opening his eyes, he stared at the clock on the bedstand. They had only an hour left before they must return to base. His grip on her tightened, and he buried his head against her damp apricot-scented hair, trying to quell the raging fear that palled his happiness. Matt Travis's gaunt face rose in front of him, and Bram struggled to shake the fear. Would he end up like Matt? A ghost of a man because the woman he loved was dead?

10

Storm and Bram sat sweating in the cockpit of the helicopter, waiting for the FBI agent with a portable radio in hand to give them the signal to lift off. The two support helicopters sat at the base of the hills in a small clearing ringed by tall graceful palms. Perspiration trickled down beneath Storm's armpits, and she wriggled around, trying to scratch various spots. It was impossible with the uncomfortable bulletproof vest on, and she finally gave up. The sweltering Bahamian sun broiled overhead, sending the temperature in the cockpit well into the nineties.

"Come on," Bram snarled softly under his breath, "let's get this show on the road."

Storm glanced back. Five FBI agents sat silently with shotguns and submachine guns at their sides. Baseball caps were pulled down across their narrowed eyes, and they, too, wore bulletproof vests. They were dressed in the standard Coast Guard apparel of a dark navy shirt and slacks. All appeared blank-faced; all kept their thoughts to themselves. Before boarding, Storm had grabbed an opportunity to draw Matt aside, hugging him and begging him to be careful. Worriedly she turned around and faced forward, catching Bram's blazing blue gaze. Everyone was uptight.

"CG 1446 and 2241, crank it up!" came the orders through the helmets they wore.

"Roger, Kingbird," Bram returned on the radio. He shot a look over to Storm. "Let's get this over with," he said flatly.

The H-52 shuddered briefly when engaging the rotor. The blades began to whirl lazily above them, moving faster and faster until finally the din increased as Storm turned the speed selector toward takeoff power. The plan was to remain hidden behind the hills ringing the bay where the *La Ceiba* lay anchored. The two helicopters would fly low-level, hugging the slopes, and then crest and roar down the other side, surprising everyone in the cove. At that moment, the SES cutters were to come around the corner of the bay at full speed and close the noose around the drug runners' activities.

Storm pulled down the shaded Plexiglas visor, covering the upper two-thirds of her face. Bram did the same, his mouth remaining a grim flat line. On this trip, Merlin had been left behind. Bram would have to be the one to shut the sliding door after the five agents were dropped onto the deck of the *La Ceiba*.

She concentrated on flying the 52 close to the hundreds of acres of Australian pine carpeting the chain of hills below them. Trees skimmed below the wheels and sponsons of the 52 as she urged the helo to remain steady. Around the hill, shifting winds created vortexes. Storm monitored the helicopter sensitively, adjusting to allow for the ebb and flow of the air currents around them. Behind them, Kyle Armstrong flew in tight formation with their aircraft. Tension permeated the interior of the ship. Bram reported their position, and Storm heard Kingbird give them the go-ahead on cresting the chain of moundlike hills to commence their airborne ambush of the *La Ceiba.*

"T minus thirty seconds," Bram reported to the one agent who had on a pair of earphones. "We're cresting . . . *now!*"

The agents locked and loaded their weapons in a simultaneous gesture.

The 52 snaked across the steepest hill. They got their first look at Chisholm Bay, its clear turquoise and emerald waters looking calm and peaceful. The *La Ceiba* lolled at the deepest point in the center of the bay. It was surrounded by more than fifty to seventy-five smaller craft ranging in size from small motorboats to sixty-foot yachts. It reminded Storm of a queen bee paid court by all her drones. The *La Ceiba* was a two-hundred-foot-class vessel with a helicopter landing pad located at the aft end of the ship.

"They see us," Bram warned.

Sure enough, the smaller boats began to move with frenetic activity, as if someone had thrown a rock into a quiet pool and the ripples were surging outward from it. The crewmen aboard the *La Ceiba* frantically pointed skyward, and Storm saw a detachment of them appearing out of the holds, rifles in hand. She broke out in a sweat.

"Sonofabitch," Bram snarled. "Kingbird, this is CG 1446. We're facing a hot landing zone. Crewmen on the *La Ceiba* are armed with M-16s and what appears to be AK-47s."

"Roger, CG 1446, we are apprised of the situation. SES *Osprey* and *Sea Hawk* will draw their fire. Out."

"Like hell they will!" Bram swore, clenching his teeth.

"Bram, just keep your hands and feet close to the controls," Storm pleaded, the anxiety in her voice reflecting the fear she felt. "If one of us gets hit going in or coming out, we've got to get the 52 up and away. We can't crash into the ship."

Bram's nostrils flared, and he gently wrapped his hands around the second set of controls.

Storm's heart pounded heavily in her chest, sweat bathing her tense body as she banked the 52 sharply, aiming for the *La Ceiba*. Matt was going to jump off straight into a withering wall of fire. Dear God, he could be killed! She shut out all those thoughts, concentrating on making a swift, accurate approach. There was nothing she could do when she saw the crew point their rifles at them. Were they going to shoot? Or were they bluffing? Her throat tightened, squelching the scream that wanted to tear from within her. She heard shouts and orders coming from the rear but was unable to turn and look. She brought the 52 flaring in with the tail dipping, and then set it down quickly on the landing pad. The door slid open, and screaming erupted all around them. Storm heard Bram shout a warning. But it was too late.

Bram had twisted around, watching as the last agent leaped from the helicopter. The earphones were jammed with a multitude of voices and orders. Jesus! this was worse than landing in a combat zone in Nam! As he spun back around, his eyes widened. He yelled for Storm to take off. The boats all around the ship were in utter panic. A forty-foot inboard motorboat careened drunkenly between smaller ones. In an attempt to escape, it lost control, slamming into the aft end of the mother ship, and exploded into a fiery ball. Then he heard Storm cry out.

There was no time to wait, look, or try to help her. To his horror, as he wrenched back on the controls to lift off, Storm slumped forward in her seat. Blood. God, it was splattered across her face. He felt the sting of several shrapnel wounds caused by the shattering glass along his neck and lower jaw. The 52 surged upward to escape the holocaust enveloping the aft end of the *La Ceiba*.

"Storm!" he yelled, risking a glance over at her. He saw her move, weakly raise one hand toward her head. Her visor had been shattered; blood covered the left side of her face.

The 52 suddenly lurched, and Bram heard a high pitched whine screech through the cockpit, warning him that something was terribly wrong. They were losing power rapidly; the 52 was sinking downward. The helicopter's rotor and tail assembly had taken shrapnel from the explosion and the collision of the boats. The foot pedals felt mushy beneath his booted feet. Land. They had to land! Bram's eyes narrowed as he labored to keep them airborne.

"Storm! Wake up!" he yelled, manipulating the controls.

Storm was groggy, pain lancing her left temple. She felt the uneven motion of the helicopter around her. Something was drastically wrong. She smelled hot oil burning. The stench acted like smelling salts on her numbed senses.

"Mayday, Mayday, Kingbird," Bram called hoarsely, "CG 1446, Mayday. We're hit. Going down on the beach. Mayday—"

The engine quit. The 52, which was limping along at one-thousand feet, suddenly started to drop toward the glistening white sands of the beach below. Autorotation! Grimly Bram shoved the collective full down, the pitch flat so that the rotors would continue to spin and give the copter some lift so they wouldn't fall like a rock and crash. He had thirty seconds to react and make lifesaving decisions before the helo would hit the beach. Glancing around, Bram selected a clear area of beach on which to land, noticing several men coming ashore. Dammit, they were smugglers! First he had to get them down in one piece.

The 52 glided heavily downward, the *whap, whap, whap* of the rotor blades using the cushion of air to ride upon. He jockeyed the 52 into the wind. At one-hundred-forty feet, Bram pulled the cyclic back. Instantly the nose came up and the ship flared, the tail rotor assembly almost brushing the sand. The flare would slow the forward motion of the helicopter, hopefully easing it down to zero knots. The ground raced up to meet them. At the last second, Bram leveled out the 52 and pulled the collective up to get all the lift he could. The helicopter settled with a shuddering thud on the beach, the rotors slowly circling to a halt above them.

Yanking off the confines of the harness, Bram turned anxiously to Storm. She was semiconscious, eyes half-closed. Nearby voices and shouts approached. Bram cursed richly, jerking around. No more than a half-mile away a band of smugglers was running toward them. Why the hell hadn't they been given weapons to defend themselves! He heard volleys of gunfire all across Chisholm Bay. Shoving the visor up into his helmet, Bram knelt at Storm's side. His mind raced with options: Maybe Armstrong could rescue them, or . . .

"Storm?" he gasped, breathing hard.

She frowned, putting her hand against her temple. "I—I'm okay, I think," she answered weakly.

Bram pushed the button on the cyclic, calling for Armstrong.

"Roger, CG 1446. I'm on my way," Kyle answered.

"Come on," he told her, unsnapping her harness, "we're getting out of here."

Bram pushed what was left of her shattered visor back up into her helmet and then put his arm around her waist, dragging her back through the cabin toward the opened door. He heard the rapidly approaching 52 in the distance above the gunfire and chaos. Storm could barely stand, and he knelt down, throwing her across his shoulder. The sand was deep, and he sank into it as he slogged his way around the 52 toward a stretch of beach where Armstrong could land.

Just as Armstrong's 52 came within a quarter-mile of where Bram stood waiting with Storm, the drug smugglers opened up with a blistering volley of gunfire. Bram watched in shock as the 52 had to abort its rescue attempt, banking sharply back out toward the bay. This was one time when gunships would have been in order. Storm sagged against him, and he divided his attention between her and the smugglers, who were closing the distance between them.

Their leader, an American with flaming red hair and a neatly kept beard, reached them first. The ugly snout of his pistol lifted toward Bram.

"Don't move or you'll both be dead," he barked.

Bram froze, keeping his arm around Storm.

"Search them!"

"We're unarmed," Bram hurled back.

"Sure, you are," a black-haired man grumbled. He rapidly ran his hands over Bram and then closely examined Storm. "What the hell—" He leaned over to get a better look. "Hey, Frank, it's a woman! I'll be damned!"

The red-haired Frank smirked. "Search her anyway. She's a Coastie."

Bram's arm snaked out. He jerked the smuggler up by the collar just as he reached forward to search Storm. "Don't touch her," he snarled, releasing the smuggler and propelling him backward into the sand. Bram jerked his head toward Frank. "She's wounded. I need to get her to a doctor—"

"Tough luck, Coastie. Ramón, get up! Come on, let's head inland." His brown eyes narrowed on Bram. "This is real Providence. You two are gonna provide us a way out of this situation. Get moving!"

The one named Ramón was small by comparison with Bram. He picked up his gun, glaring at the Coast Guard officer as he approached them. Shoving the gun in Bram's heavily muscled back, he snapped, "Move!"

Storm became aware of jagged motion, her head aching as though someone had slugged her with a baseball bat. It was hot, and she felt the damp stickiness of her flight suit chafing roughly against her skin. Someone was carrying her in his arms. She heard voices, but they blurred in and out as she lingered between levels of consciousness. Finally they halted, and she felt herself being lowered to the ground. Someone was gently removing the heavy helmet from her head. A cooling breeze brought her around, and she forced her eyes open. Bram's grim features danced before her eyes. It took several long minutes to realize he had propped her up against the trunk of a pine tree.

Bram's face drew closer and she blinked, dazed. He drew his handkerchief from his pocket and gently wiped the blood from her cheek and jaw below the wound she had sustained. Every touch hurt, and she tried not to wince.

"Sorry," he whispered gruffly. "Just lie still and don't talk."

Frank and his four fellow smugglers rested under another tree, guarding them. Getting to his feet, the leader wandered over to them. He looked down at the woman, interest in his eyes. A slight smile curved at his thin mouth.

"I didn't know you Coasties were sending women to do your dirty work now," he said.

Bram ignored him, concentrating on Storm's head wound. He picked up her helmet, his heart plummeting. A stray piece of shrapnel had smashed through her visor just above her left eyebrow, glancing off her skull and lodging in the helmet itself. She had come within a centimeter of dying. Sweat dripped from his jaw as he examined the wound. It was a small cut no more than an inch in length, but scalp wounds always bled heavily.

"She ain't bad lookin' once you get her cleaned up. What's her name?"

Bram twisted his head, glowering up at him in silent warning to back off.

Frank simpered and leaned over, reading the black leather patch emblazoned with her name and rank on her flight suit. "Lt. Storm Travis. She live up to her name, Coastie?"

Bram gritted his teeth, sensing that silence was the better part of valor for the moment, and returned his attention to Storm. She was groggy, and he needed water for both of them. Keeping a steadying hand on her arm, he worriedly watched her struggle to become more conscious. Frank finally grew bored and walked away. Drawing in a shaky breath, Bram offered Storm a tense smile.

"How do you feel?"

Storm cleared her throat. "Terrible. I've never had such a splitting headache. What happened?"

He recounted the chain of events for her in a lowered voice. Storm's eyes narrowed with pain. She slowly sat up, cradling her head in her hands.

"Kyle couldn't land?"

"No. These guys started firing."

"Then, we're prisoners."

"Yeah," he said flatly, glaring at the sand. Taking off

his helmet, he ran his fingers through his wet hair in disgust.

"What do you think they'll do?"

"The ringleader, Frank, said we're their ticket out of here."

"That's good," Storm said, peering up. "At least they won't kill us yet." Her lips parted when she realized he was wounded also. "Glass?" she asked, reaching over and gently touching his right cheek.

Bram nodded. "Yeah, we both look like pin cushions. That shrapnel from the collision must have ricocheted when it hit the cockpit glass, and then struck you." His voice grew strained. "God, I was never so scared as when I looked over and saw your face covered with blood."

Storm reached out, touching his hand. "I'm sorry, Bram."

Grimacing, he continued to squat by her side. "Nothing to apologize for, princess. I knew something was going to happen today. I could feel it coming."

"I did too," she admitted rawly, "but I didn't want to say anything. There was nothing we could do about it anyway, Bram."

He sucked in air between his clenched teeth. "Next time I do this, I'm going in with a pistol or an M-16. If we had either this time, we might have escaped."

Storm scanned the group. "Not with five rifles staring down our throats, Bram. They would have killed us outright." She took his handkerchief and wiped away the last of the blood on her cheek. "As it stands, we may have a chance to survive this."

"Maybe," Bram concurred gloomily. "The leader has eyes for you. I'm more worried about that than anything else."

"Let's play it by ear. These guys don't have that kind of time to do much else other than make a run for it, much less think about attacking me."

His eyes glittered dangerously. "They won't lay a hand on you," he promised.

Ramón came over, motioning for them to get to their feet. Storm struggled to stand, momentarily dizzy. She was grateful for Bram's arm around her waist, steadying her. For the next hour, they climbed the slope of the hill, weaving through the pines and palm trees. Storm regained most of her strength during that time and preceded Bram. They came across a small stream. Gratefully Storm knelt down, splashing the cooling water across her face and neck. The water tasted delicious as she scooped it up in her cupped hands, allowing it to trickle down her parched throat. She longed to strip out of the smelly flight suit and cleanse her sweaty body.

"Take five," Frank ordered them. He strode over to where Storm and Bram were sitting. His dark brown eyes narrowed in on Storm, and he halted a few feet from her. Bram rose slowly to his feet, his legs spread slightly apart, hands hanging tensely at his sides.

"Don't try it, Coastie," Frank cautioned menacingly. "Get over there and sit down. I'm just going to talk to your girlfriend here."

Bram hesitated.

"Move," Frank warned.

Storm's eyes widened with silent pleading for Bram to do as he was told. Bram reluctantly walked over to a tree and leaned against it, vigilantly watching them. She returned her attention to the smuggler, who came and crouched near where she was kneeling.

"Just to show you there're no hard feelings, I'm Frank Carter."

"I doubt if you're interested in my feelings, Carter," she snapped quietly, her eyes blazing.

He grinned broadly. "I like a woman with spirit. Storm's a real good name for you. How you feeling?"

"Like hell. How am I supposed to feel?"

He shrugged, pursing his lips. "When you play with the big boys, honey, it gets rough sometimes."

"I don't regret an instant of it, Carter."

His smile faded. "You're the best surprise of this whole miserable fiasco, you know that? I could make it real easy on you, honey. Why don't you join up with us? We're going to escape. It's just a matter of waiting for night to fall and then making it to one of the bays and paying for a ride to Nassau." He reached out, his hand extended to touch her. With blinding speed, Storm struck out, slapping his face. The slap resounded like a shot. Leaping to her feet with practiced ease, Storm watched as Carter slowly rose, his face red.

"Don't touch me," she rasped. "I hate you and I hate your kind, Carter."

He nursed his cheek, sizing her up. "Real spitfire, aren't you, Travis? Well, we'll see what you're really made of tonight."

Bram came over to where she was standing as Carter stalked off. She was trembling from the rush of adrenaline and closed her eyes for a moment. She felt Bram's reassuring hand on her arm.

"Okay?" he asked, worriedly searching her wan features.

"Fine. Just a little shaky. The bastard. . . ."

"What did he say?"

Storm watched as Carter goaded his party back to their feet, swearing loudly at them. "Apparently he has plans for me tonight after we make camp."

Bram's mouth tightened. "We've got to try and escape, Storm."

"Carter isn't the type to attack me in front of everyone. He's too insecure for that. If he leads me off at gunpoint, maybe I can disarm him."

"That's too risky."

"Do you have a better plan?"

Bram shook his head. "Not right at the moment."

By nightfall, they were well on the other side of the hill boundary line and working their way down to Red Bay. What had taken a few minutes by helicopter had taken them half a day on foot to cover. Carter wasn't stupid; he ordered their hands tied in front of them and separated them. There was no opportunity to escape, and when they finally began to make camp, Storm wearily sank to her knees, leaning back against a tree. Her head spun with questions. Was Matt safe? Had Kyle been able to radio back for help and alert the authorities that they had been captured? Would they send a party to try and rescue them? Carter had been giving her insidious looks all afternoon. Storm yearned to be next to Bram. Just his nearness was a source of invisible support to her.

Lying down, Storm closed her eyes, trying to rest. If Carter was going to attack her, she would need every ounce of reserve in a battle of wits and human strength to fight him off. Hot tears pricked the back of her eyes as she lay there. She loved Bram so much, her heart ached with the pain of what he must be feeling right now. She had seen the fear in his eyes for her safety. Swallowing against a lump in her throat, Storm forced herself to rest . . . and wait.

Storm was roughly shaken awake. She blinked, feeling a hand dig harshly into her shoulder, yanking her into a sitting position. It was dark. Only pale slats of moonlight filtered haphazardly down through the pine trees to drive the surrounding pitch blackness away.

"Come on," Carter growled softly, jerking her to her feet, "you and I have some unfinished business to attend to."

Her heart pounded achingly in her chest as she struggled momentarily. Carter's fingers dug deeply into her upper arm, bruising her flesh. Bram! Where was he? Eyes widening, Storm tried to twist around to catch sight of him. Their eyes met for an agonizing split second. Storm saw the terror in Bram's face as he struggled against the ropes that bound him hand and foot. Not only that, but they had gagged him as well. Nausea rose in her throat as Carter shoved her forward into the thick underbrush. She nearly lost her balance, stumbling awkwardly. At the last second, Carter gripped her arm, jerking her upright.

"What's the matter, honey? Scared?"

She had to think! No matter how frightened she was, she had to think! Storm looked around at the dark, shadowed foliage. She needed a small space to operate within. Just a small one! Frank held the gun close to his side, occasionally jabbing it into her ribs as he forced her deeper into the lush forest. Branches and leaves swatted her, and Storm felt their sting against her unprotected face. Her throat was constricted in pain, and her breathing was harsh and labored. Revulsion coursed through her. Bram couldn't help her.

They broke into a small clearing dappled with moonlight. Storm worked frantically at the ropes that bit cruelly into her flesh. If only she could free herself!

"That's far enough," Carter said ominously.

Her heartbeat accelerated, pounding thunderously in her chest. Slowly Storm turned toward him, her nostrils flared, her body tensed.

He grinned, motioning for her to come closer. In that single gesture, Carter had waved his right hand out away from his body for a split second. And it was just such a move that Storm had been praying for. In one unbroken motion, she lifted her right leg, aiming her steel-toed flight boot at Carter's hand. There was a metallic snap as boot met gun. Carter yelped, his fingers torn loose from the gun, the revolver sailing off into the darkness.

Storm completed the spinning circle, planting both feet firmly on the ground, breathing hard. Carter snarled an obscenity, holding his wrist.

"You broke it!" he rasped. "You bitch; you broke my wrist!"

He made a lunge for her. Storm again lifted her leg, her boot colliding solidly with Carter's jaw. There was the distinct sound of bone crunching beneath the power of her kick. Carter was thrown backward, uttering a groan as he crumpled into an unconscious heap.

She had lost her balance with her hands tied. Storm saw the ground coming up fast and tucked her head, allowing her shoulder to take the brunt of the jolt. Hitting the earth, she rolled over on her back. A gasp escaped her. Out of nowhere a man dressed in camouflage fatigues pressed his hand across her mouth to stop her from screaming. Storm's eyes widened in shock.

"Shh! It's me, Matt."

Gradually he eased his hand from her mouth. Storm sobbed for breath as she anxiously looked up at her brother. His face was shaded with green, black, and brown tones. The jungle fatigues he wore blended perfectly with the backdrop of the night surrounding them. Miraculously Storm saw four more men melt out of the shadows to kneel by her. One of them hand-cuffed Carter's arms behind him and placed a gag in his mouth in case he regained consciousness.

Matt unsheathed a Ka-Bar, a knife used in jungle warfare, quickly slicing the ropes binding her wrists. Helping his sister sit up, he held her until she stopped trembling.

"Okay?" he asked in a hoarse whisper.

Storm gulped. "Y-yes. Thank God you're—"

"Bram? Is he still alive?"

She blinked back tears. "Yes." She pointed to her left. "There're four other smugglers with him, Matt. They've got him bound and gagged."

Matt's mouth tautened, his eyes gleaming like obsidian. "Okay, you stay put. We'll do the rest." He silently rose to his full height, giving her a worried look. "You all right?"

Nodding, Storm wiped the tears from her cheeks. "Just scared."

Matt gave a quiet order, and the men blended back into the shadows, melding into forest once again. Storm rose to her knees, unsure whether she could stand. What if there was a gunfight? Bram and Matt could be killed! Tears caught in her throat as she sat there, fists clenched against her thighs, waiting.

Within ten minutes, the smugglers had been captured without a shot being fired. Matt came back to the clearing, his face slightly more relaxed. He held out his hand, helping Storm stand, and led her back along the path.

"Bram's okay," he said in a normal tone of voice. "Angry as hell, but okay."

Storm smiled shakily, her legs wobbly. She leaned against Matt. "This was too close," she whispered, her voice sounding raw.

"I know."

"How did it go aboard the ship?"

"Hotter than hell. One man was wounded, but we captured the number-two man in Garcia's organization besides the largest haul of coke ever." He gave her a bleak smile. "That makes me one step closer to Garcia himself. Now all I have to do is track him down in his lair, which is on the Texas gulf coast."

Storm barely heard her brother's words as she caught sight of Bram. They had just untied him, and he was stiffly getting to his feet. He saw her. She left her brother's protective embrace and flew to him. Bram wrapped his arms tightly around her, drawing her against him. A sob tore from her, and Storm buried her head on his chest, eyes tightly shut.

"Oh, Bram," she cried, "I was so worried—"

He kissed her hair. "I'm okay. Are you?" he asked thickly, assessing her worriedly.

She didn't know whether to laugh or cry. "I'm fine . . . fine . . ." Her charcoal eyes were large and vulnerable like a child's. "I was so scared," she sobbed, melting back into his embrace.

Bram groaned, holding her tightly, feeling her warmth, her strength. "Thank God," he whispered rawly. "I've never felt so damned helpless. Never." Tears brimmed his eyes as he buried his head next to hers. The rage and impotence he had experienced when Carter took her into the jungle had nearly strangled him. The smugglers had known he would try to prevent Storm from being taken by Carter. By binding and gagging him, they had taken no chances. In the ensuing moments after she had disappeared into the darkness with Carter, he had wanted to scream. Scream with frustration and pure, unadulterated rage over what Carter could do to Storm.

Hearing someone approach, Bram raised his head. He gave Matt a grateful look.

"I think we're ready to go," Matt told them, giving his sister a solicitous glance. "We've got two helicopters coming in to pick us up in a meadow near here."

"Sounds good. We owe you a lot, Matt."

Matt smiled grudgingly and touched Storm's shoulder. "Couldn't let my big sister down, could I? We have a doctor waiting for you in Nassau. A shower, change of clothes, and a hot meal at a hotel will put you back in order."

"Nassau?" Bram asked, mystified.

"Cutters are overcrowded with prisoners right now.

We get the ritz tonight. Tomorrow we'll be flown back to Miami."

It was almost eleven P.M. before they were medically attended to and then dropped off at a hotel in Nassau. Storm felt the stares of people in the lobby as well as the clerks behind the desk. They must look a sight in their dirtied flight suits and disheveled appearance, she thought tiredly. Bram seemed supremely unaware of it. Getting the key, he guided her to the bank of elevators with his hand resting on her elbow.

"Looks like we'll be the talk of the hotel," he said, smiling slightly as they rode the elevator to the tenth floor.

Storm grimaced. "Ask me if I care at this point."

"Do you care, Lieutenant Travis?"

She warmed to his teasing, following him out of the elevator and down the plushly carpeted hall. "Not in the least, Lieutenant Gallagher. We're paid to do a job, not look pretty."

Bram grinned, his sky-blue eyes glimmering with hungry intensity as he scrutinized her. "You look beautiful no matter what you do or don't wear, lady." He slipped the key into the lock, opening the door. "Grab the bathroom first," he urged. "I'll order us up some food. I'm starved."

Storm shook her head ruefully, a smile touching her lips. "Always thinking of your stomach first," she sighed in mock exasperation.

Bram closed the door and took her into his arms. Leaning down, he gently kissed her lips. "I was thinking first about loving you as soon as we get cleaned up."

The tension surrounding their narrow escape began to subside, and Storm managed a laugh. "You're impossible!"

He molded his mouth to her lips and felt her responding pressure as the heat rapidly escalated between

them. She tasted of warmth. They were alive. . . .
Placing a rein on his spiraling desires, Bram drew away,
a feral light flaming in his azure eyes. "Get in the tub
before I carry you over to the bed," he warned.

Shaken by the intensity of his voice, Storm nodded.
They had come very close to death, and the sudden
look that shadowed his eyes made her poignantly
aware of just how much she loved Bram. "I love you."

Long slanting rays of sun invaded their room. Storm
stirred, nuzzling like a lost kitten beneath Bram's chin.
Eyes still heavy with sleep, she forced them open.
Yesterday's events slowly seeped into her waking state.
She automatically slid her arm across Bram's powerful
chest, giving him a hug. Last night they had showered,
eaten a quick meal, and literally fallen into bed, exhausted. Relishing the hard, warm strength of his naked
body against her own, Storm sighed contentedly.

Bram moved his hand downward, lightly stroking her
back and hips, sending a liquid message throughout her
sensitized nervous system. Automatically Storm pressed
the full length of her body against him in reaction. A
low purr came from deep within her throat as his
skillful hand stroked the sensitive flesh of her inner
thigh.

"Good morning," he greeted huskily, raising himself
up on one elbow.

A tremulous smile tinged her lips as she opened
her eyes, meeting his and stirring beneath his gaze.
"It is," she sighed, sliding her hands up across his
arms to his well-muscled shoulders, reveling in his
masculine strength. He was so alive, so vital, it made
her heart sing in unison with her throbbing, waking
body.

His face was relaxed, his features almost boyish, a
rebellious lock of hair dipping down on his smooth

brow. Storm reached up, taming the tendril back in place, luxuriating in the scent of him. Longing burned in the depths of his eyes as he leaned down and caressed her lips as if she were some fragile, delicate rose to be worshipped.

"Mmm, you smell good. . . . Like apricots and honey," he murmured, nibbling at her lip, placing several tiny lingering kisses at the corners and then allowing her to feel the masculine strength of his mouth as he molded it possessively against her. She was tautly strung, responding to each featherlike graze of his hand. He brushed his palm provocatively across her nipples, hearing her moan with pleasure. Dragging his mouth from her lips, he tasted each one, tugging gently, feeling her stiffen with desire for him.

Bram became lost in the sensuousness of the moment and was aware of her wonderful feminine scent that was an aphrodisiac to his own heightened arousal. She tasted like sweet clover honey to him, and her flesh was warm smooth jade to be tantalized by his exploration. From the day he had met her, Storm had never been any less than all woman to him. She possessed a courage coupled with a sensitivity that left him shaken and in awe. She was life to him in all respects, all ways, and he never wanted to lose her. He loved her. Drawing her beneath him, he parted her thighs, wanting, needing to share the power of his feelings with her alone. A groan came from within him as he plunged into the welcoming depths of her liquid warmth. They were one. She was life—giving, taking, and sharing without reserve—and he guided her through levels of euphoria, leaving them both satiated and breathless in its torrid wake.

Storm trembled deliciously as Bram drew her protectively against him afterward. She kissed him, tasting the salt of perspiration on his cheek. He returned the kiss, his mouth caressing her lips in tender adoration. An ache of joy filled her heart, until she was at a loss for words.

Bram stroked her hair, running the gossamer threads through his fingers. "You're like silk," he told her, his voice laden with spent passion.

Storm smiled contentedly, tilting her head up to bask luxuriantly in the warmth of his love. "I always thought of myself as good old durable cotton—infinitely practical, natural, and something that could be worn forever."

He cocked an eyebrow. "No," he retorted mildly, brushing her flushed cheek lightly, "you're silk. Exotic, unique, beautiful . . ."

"Hmm, I never saw myself that way before."

"I do. Besides, silk is a natural fiber like cotton, and it wears forever." He traced her brow, nose, and touched her rosy, well-kissed lips. "And like silk, you require special attention in the care and handling department."

She giggled. "You mean you can't just throw me into any old washing machine?"

"Nope. Special treatment for you, my lady."

Her gray eyes shimmered with joy as she rose up on one elbow and imprinted a kiss on his mouth. "I never thought of myself as an expensive cut of cloth, Lieutenant Gallagher. Do you always perceive the world in such an interesting fashion?"

"Is that a pun, Lieutenant Travis soon-to-be Lieutenant Gallagher?"

She braced her arms against his chest, laughter edging up the corners of her mouth. "I'll settle for Travis-Gallagher."

He grinned. "Do it this way—when things are going right, use Travis. But when things are going badly, use Gallagher."

Their laughter filled the room. Bram ran his hands down the length of her long back. He gradually sobered, drowning in her lovely dove-gray eyes. "I love you, Storm," he told her quietly. He struggled with words that normally came easily to his glib tongue. But this morning they didn't. He was overwhelmed with her effortlessness and her ability to share her happiness with him. "When you got injured, I died inside," he admitted, meeting her serious gaze. "I've never felt so torn up. I had a helicopter that was dying on me, and you were leaning forward in the harness with blood streaming down the side of your face." He shut his eyes, fighting to arrest the surge of emotion accompanying that gruesome picture. Releasing a shaky sigh, Bram continued. "Storm, I didn't know what real love was until I met you. I thought I knew. I had based a marriage on those concepts. But they were wrong. Your honesty, your forthrightness, taught me the happiness of actually sharing my life with you. And it wasn't painful."

Storm swallowed against tears as she caressed his cheek. "Love is always interwoven with pain, Bram. We can't have one without the other. But with the way we feel toward one another, I know our love will outdistance any pain we might cause one another."

He grimaced. "I was scared. Scared that I'd lose you like your brother lost his wife. Matt's haunted. I see it in his eyes: I can see it in his expression. I sat there tied up, watching you sleep while those smugglers were eyeing you. I saw myself in Matt's position. If they had hurt you in any way, I would have hunted every last one of them down and made them pay—"

"Shh," she soothed, placing her fingertips against his mouth. "It didn't happen, Bram. We're alive. We're safe, and we have each other." She rested her brow against his stern, uncompromising jaw. "No one said life was particularly safe either in an emotional or a physical sense, darling. Matt reached out to embrace life by loving Maura. He paid a price for having the courage to live. And we're risk-takers in the same sense, Bram.

We're both willing to pay the price, whatever that might be, to reach out and love one another regardless of the emotional or physical cost." She leaned upward, kissing his mouth. "Do you know how many people never live at all? How many are afraid to step out of the familiar and experience things such as placing your heart in someone else's hands?"

He nodded, running his fingers through her ginger hair. "I was like that after the divorce, Storm. I met you and fell like a ton of bricks. And my feelings toward you scared the hell out of me because I was afraid to reach out and live again."

"But you did anyway, Bram. That says something about your caliber as a human being."

"And you? You weren't afraid to love me. Or were you?"

Storm lowered her lashes. "I admitted I was frightened, Bram. And I was. Hal was torn from me. I didn't think I could stand the pain of maybe losing you someday too." She gave a helpless shrug. "But the alternative wasn't acceptable."

He sat up, leaning against the headboard, gathering Storm into his arms. "Sometimes I wonder if our courage to reach out emotionally might be construed as foolhardiness by someone else. Because we won't live half-lives with one another, princess. And the more we give and share with one another, the larger the potential for pain if something happens."

"I know," she responded softly, loving his closeness, nuzzling his cheek. "The physical threat to us is far greater than the emotional one, Bram."

"Tell me about it," he agreed unhappily. "All it takes is one bullet from a drug smuggler's gun—"

"Or a malfunction aboard a helicopter. Or a bad wave. . . . Bram, in our business there're many chances for disaster. We live with those daily. We both love what we do." She looked up at him. "You wouldn't ask me to give up flying because you're afraid of losing me, would you?"

The silence was heart-stopping as he stared at her. His eyes filled with tears, and he compressed his lips. "No—no, I wouldn't ask that of you, Storm."

She nodded, on the verge of tears herself. "If you had, a huge part of me would have slowly died, Bram. I would have given it up for you, but I would have been unhappy."

He lovingly placed his finger beneath her chin. "Look at me," he commanded huskily.

Raising her head, Storm met his clear azure gaze, her heart contracting. The path of tears down his stubbled cheeks evoked a cauldron of emotions from within her. It stunned her. Hal had never cried; never shared this vulnerable human part of himself with her. But Bram trusted her . . . loved her enough to share this secret side of himself with her. A small cry escaped her parted lips.

"I want you to be yourself, princess. To ask you to give up your career would be like asking me to do the same thing. And I know you'd never do that, Storm. I can do no less for you." He cupped her face, gently drawing her forward until their lips barely brushed. "Part of the reason I love you so much is because you're all that you can be. You haven't let society tell you it's wrong to join the service, fly a helicopter, or even risk your life. And you're woman enough to cry when it's all over. That makes me feel good, Storm—I cherish your ability to run to my arms and be held. You're not pretending to be a superwoman. You're simply yourself, and God, woman, I love you for that and I always will."

**An epic novel of exotic rituals
and the lure of the Upper Amazon**

THE
TAKERS
RIVER
OF GOLD

JERRY AND S.A. AHERN

THE TAKERS are the intrepid Josh Culhane and the seductive Mary Mulrooney. These two adventurers launch an incredible journey into the Brazilian rain forest. Far upriver, the jungle yields its deepest secret—the lost city of the Amazon warrior women!

THE TAKERS series is making publishing history. Awarded *The Romantic Times* first prize for High Adventure in 1984, the opening book in the series was hailed by *The Romantic Times* as "the next trend in romance writing and reading. Highly recommended!"

Jerry and S.A. Ahern have never been better!

TAK-3

For the woman who expects a little more out of love, get Silhouette Special Edition.

Take 4 books free – no strings attached.

If you yearn to experience more passion and pleasure in your romance reading ... to share even the most private moments of romance and sensual love between spirited heroines and their ardent lovers, then Silhouette Special Edition has everything you've been looking for.

Get 6 books each month before they are available anywhere else!

Act now and we'll send you four exciting Silhouette Special Edition romance novels. They're our gift to introduce you to our convenient home subscription service. Every month, we'll send you six new passion-filled Special Edition books. Look them over for 15 days. If you keep them, pay just $11.70 for all six. Or return them at no charge.

We'll mail your books to you *two full months before they are available* anywhere else. Plus, with every shipment, you'll receive the Silhouette Books Newsletter absolutely free. *And with Silhouette Special Edition there are never any shipping or handling charges.*

Mail the coupon today to get your four free books — and more romance than you ever bargained for.

Silhouette Special Edition is a service mark and a registered trademark.